MOM'S LAST WISH
CHARLENE NEIL

ALSO BY CHARLENE NEIL

SINGLE STORIES

The Presence

MOM'S LAST WISH

CHARLENE NEIL

Affinity
Rainbow Publications

2024

Mom's Last Wish
© 2024 by Charlene Neil

Affinity E-Book Press NZ LTD
Canterbury, New Zealand

1st Edition

ISBN: 978-1-99-104057-2 (paperback)
ISBN: 978-1-99-104058-9 (EPUB)
ISBN: 978-1-99-104059-6 (PDF)
ISBN: 978-1-99-104060-2 (KINDLE)

Editor: Angela Koenig
Proof Editor: Lisa M
Cover Design: Irish Dragon Designs
Production Design: Affinity Publication Services

ACKNOWLEDGMENTS

I would like to express my sincere gratitude to Amy Saunders for her invaluable contribution to the writing of *Mom's Last Wish*. Amy's guidance, expertise, and unwavering support have been instrumental in shaping the content of this book. Her keen sense of humor also played a crucial role in delineating the characters, enabling them to shine in their truest form. Thank you, Amy, for your dedicated collaboration and for adding your unique touch to this project.

I would like to extend my heartfelt gratitude to Julie Dragon at Affinity Rainbow Publications for her unwavering support and belief in me throughout the creation of this book. Julie's encouragement and guidance have been invaluable, and her belief in my ability to bring this story to life has been a constant source of inspiration. Thank you, Julie, for your continued support and for being a driving force behind this project.

DEDICATION

This book is lovingly dedicated to my daughter, Amy Saunders. Your unwavering support, guidance, and collaborative spirit have been instrumental in bringing *Mom's Last Wish* to life. Your contributions and presence throughout the writing process have made this journey truly meaningful and enjoyable. Thank you for being an inspiration in both writing and life. This book is forever dedicated to you.

TABLE OF CONTENTS

CHAPTER ONE

Lucy sighed as she shuffled aching feet down the long passage toward the night matron's office. When she stopped at the open door to the sterile white room, she saw her sitting behind her desk, staring at her computer screen. Her boyish good looks set Lucy's heart racing, galloping as if it had somewhere else to be. She was tall and athletic with short dark hair, tanned skin, and a deep husky voice. *Maybe a little too butch for my taste,* Lucy mused, but her eyes couldn't help but wander down to her chest which, to her delightful surprise, was flat. But the matron's brown eyes seemed annoyed, and Lucy wasn't in the mood for trouble.

"You wanted to see me, Matron?" She felt nervous and her breath got caught in her throat and she swallowed.

"Sister Donald." Matron Sally Smith's voice was stern with more than a hint of irritation. "Sit." She pointed at the empty chair across from her pine desk.

Lucy obliged and sank down shakily. "Is something wrong, Matron?" She inhaled slowly as she wrestled to calm her nerves. After a night that seemed intent on carrying on for what felt like forever, Matron Smith intimidated her a little more than she cared to admit. At three am, with four more hours left of her shift, she wanted nothing more than for the long night to come to an end.

"You're the team leader and I noticed all your staff reported late for work. Care to explain?" She spoke in a stern voice, asserting her dominance.

"Sally... Sorry, I mean, Matron, you know I don't usually work nights..."

"And?"

"I really don't know this team. You'll have to give me some time to become more familiar with them."

Matron Smith's frosty glare grew even colder than Lucy thought possible. "You had sex with a patient."

"It was consensual," she objected, trying to defend what little honor she hoped she had left. "And it was only after she was discharged from the hospital. So technically she wasn't a patient anymore." A memory flashed of the painfully short relationship she'd had with Jude, the charming young lady she'd been nursing in the ICU. Jude had taken Lucy on a date, which Lucy had reluctantly

2

accepted, only to be ghosted after one night of passion. Unfortunately, the hospital manager found out when Lucy had stupidly posted about it on social media, and she was brought in for a disciplinary hearing. Night shift was her penance. She was lucky they didn't fire her.

"It was unprofessional," the matron snapped. "Placing you on night shift is your only punishment and I expect you to take charge of your unit properly."

"I'm sorry, Matron. I will have a chat with my team." Lucy sighed and rolled her eyes. She hated working with people she didn't know.

"Dismissed." The matron raised her hand and waved toward the office door as her attention was drawn back to her computer monitor.

As Lucy stood, her eye caught the computer screen. It was switched off. Thankful that the session with the matron was over, she rushed from her office to her designated ward for the next seven nights. She found the three nurses on duty were fast asleep in their chairs at the nurses' station.

"Guys." She spoke louder than she had intended, her voice echoing off the walls.

Nurse Carmen's head shot up and she quickly reached for the other two nurses, searching wildly for their shoulders, finally tapping them anxiously.

"Can we please work together as a team?" Lucy asked, almost begging, sounding a tad desperate.

All three of them stared at her blankly, faces pale.

"You must get to work on time and sleeping on duty is absolutely out of the question. What if something happens to one of the patients and all of you are asleep?"

Carmen cleared her throat. "Sorry, Sister Donald. It won't happen again."

The other two, Magdalene and Sophie, nodded in agreement just as a call bell rang to their left.

"Is that Mrs. Howard again?" Lucy asked, but before any of them answered, she turned and hurried to the patient's room.

Mrs. Howard mumbled into the dead space above her. "John, where are you?"

"What's wrong, Mrs. Howard?" Lucy reached over the raised bedside and gently stroked the elderly lady's creased face.

"Where's John? What have you done with my husband?" Her eyes looked sad as they filled with water.

Lucy watched as a tear escaped from her left eye and slid down her cheek. "Your husband's not here, Mrs. Howard." He had passed away about ten years ago, but it would be cruel to remind her of that. Her dementia allowed her to forget his passing, which wasn't such a bad thing.

Mrs. Howard gripped Lucy's hand with bony fingers. "He was here just a moment ago." Her eyes opened wide.

In Lucy's experience, patients sometimes saw their departed family members right before they passed on. "He's gone home to rest. I'm sure he'll be back in the morning,"

4

she lied. No point in upsetting her now since in the morning she wouldn't remember the conversation anyway.

"Oh. Okay, dear. Thank you." She let go of Lucy's hand.

Lucy tucked her in and then waited for her to go back to sleep before turning and leaving the room.

†

By the third night Lucy was bored out of her mind. Her ward accommodated a mere ten patients that night and Mrs. Howard had sadly passed away the previous day. Lucy seriously needed to find something to pass the next twelve hours, and what better way than to harass the scary night matron. Lucy had never identified as gay or straight. For personal reasons, however, she always preferred to be with women. Since that first night on night shift, Lucy had been fantasizing about the matron.

She sauntered toward her office which was at the end of the passage, all the while envisioning how she was going to seduce the impossibly cold Sally Smith. When she reached the doorway, she inhaled sharply before taking the last step. As she exhaled, she leaned seductively against the doorframe, while intertwining her fingers in front of her. When she didn't get an immediate response, Lucy cleared her throat and skillfully glanced down at her feet. She knew from experience that the butch ones liked being the hunters.

So, she would grant her that, just this once, mainly because she was bored. She slowly tucked a loose strand of her blonde hair behind her ear while carefully contemplating playful flirting.

"What is it *now*, Sister Donald?" The matron's tone suggested she'd been bothered all week. Her stare penetrated Lucy, as if looking straight through her from across her desk. The white walls in her office made the room appear lifeless. Her office had no windows, just a desk that faced the door with her on the opposite end of it, facing Lucy as she stood in the doorway. Her tone never fooled Lucy even for a second, she could sense her anxiety and noted her hands shaking slightly.

"I...err...j-just n...needed your help inserting an, err, I...IV." Lucy attempted and obviously failed at a stutter.

Matron Smith sighed. "Are you too incompetent, Sister Donald?"

"I...I...I... tried, but she's a fossil."

"A fossil?" The matron failed at hiding her smile, which had curled up slightly on one side of her mouth, and with a hint of humor in her eyes she commented, "That's a bit rude, isn't it?"

"Well, she is ninety-eight." Lucy felt the heat crawl up her face, but continued, "Her skin is paper thin and her veins have lost their elasticity. I'm sorry, I didn't mean to be rude, just trying to break the ice." Lucy feigned a shiver. She hadn't actually tried inserting the IV line yet. It was just an excuse to soften Sally up, and to draw her in to her wicked ways. If there was one thing she knew, it was how to manipulate potentially unsuspecting victims. Lucy was very comfortable in her own skin, and generally found it very easy to flirt with women.

Sally got up from her chair and openly smiled for the first time. "Okay, I'll give it a shot."

Her sudden change in demeanor made Lucy's heart leap. She hadn't noticed before, but the matron had a very sexy smile. She followed Lucy to the ward to the patient's bed. Everything had already been set up for the intravenous line. As Sally aimed the needle, Lucy purposefully leaned in to hover over her shoulder, making sure her breath moved down Sally's exposed neck. As she looked down, she could see the goose bumps forming right below her hairline. Sally stiffened, sighed, and looked up at Lucy with a frown. "You're making me nervous. Can you wait outside while I do this?"

Before Lucy turned to leave the room, she noticed Sally's hands visibly shaking. Lucy felt a slight smirk creeping across her face. She loved having this effect on anyone she found attractive.

A few minutes later, Sally emerged from the patient's room with a proud look on her face. "It's done."

"Thank you. You're really good with your hands."

Sally cleared her throat. "Anything else?"

Lucy noticed Sally's gaze lower to her lips as she spoke and felt her gut clench. *Bingo*. Now that she knew she had her attention, her mind went abuzz with a myriad of the *anything else* she could possibly help her with.

"Can I let you know?" she asked as she thoughtfully wet her lips.

Sally seemed to hesitate for a second before she spun on her heels and dashed off back to her small white cage with the blank computer screen.

Lucy found herself wondering how she did it. How she managed night after night in that tiny little office. Anyone even remotely normal would most certainly lose their mind.

"Carmen," she called to one of the junior nurses who was busy tending to a patient.

"Yes, Sister Donald?"

"I'm heading off to Matron Smith for about an hour. We have some paperwork to complete. Can you hold the fort while I'm gone?" Nurse Carmen was young and still new in the nursing field, but Lucy felt she could trust her. She was bright as a button.

"Of course, Sister Donald," Carmen answered without pause.

"Don't you dare fall asleep." Lucy raised her left arm and glanced at her watch. It was two am. "See you just after three."

"Sure, no problem."

†

As expected, she found Sally sitting behind her desk, staring at the computer screen. She wondered whether the screen was still blank. Was she doing something productive or just wasting company time on the internet, browsing or bouncing between the endless choices of social media sites? Lucy waited patiently for Sally to notice her. She was relieved to see that when Sally finally looked up, there was less annoyance in her general demeanor.

"Is there something you need?" Sally's eyes looked heavy as she broke the silence with her husky voice.

"Yes." Lucy inched through the doorway, then closed and locked the door behind her.

As Lucy edged closer to Sally, she could see the tension in her body as her fingers clenched the arms of her chair. Her knuckles were white from the pressure. With little hesitation, Lucy closed the distance between them. She could hear Sally swallow as she strategically positioned herself on the edge of the desk directly in front of her. Lifting her right foot, she placed it on the part of the chair that was exposed between Sally's legs, all the while maintaining eye contact. Sally's face turned crimson. Lucy leaned forward, placed her hands on top of Sally's tightly gripping hands, and whispered into her ear, "Breathe."

Sally inhaled slowly and exhaled shakily. Her gaze followed Lucy's lips as she leaned in lasciviously to further close the distance between their mouths. The instant their lips met, Sally seemed to lose any remaining self-control. She let go of the chair's arms, grabbed Lucy's hips, hauled herself out of the chair and stood tightly between her legs. Lucy's legs automatically wrapped around Sally's waste while her hands slipped in under her scrubs and found her hot skin. Lucy's fingers lingered on Sally's lower back, as Lucy drank in her silky skin. Sally groaned as she seductively kissed Lucy, biting her lip and slipping the tip of her tongue into her wet mouth, seemingly aching for release. Lucy took great pleasure in playing the gentle teasing game for just a moment longer. With her hands still on Lucy's hips, Sally tugged her to the edge of the desk where their groins met and ground eagerly against each other. With steady rhythmic talent she gyrated her hips against Sally's. Lucy was pleasantly surprised as her hands moved over Sally's back, and she felt the muscles contract, dancing in response to her touch. Hungrily, she gripped Sally's strong shoulder blades all the while thrusting her hips to meet her tempo.

Lucy was still seated on the desk and couldn't believe how Sally's talented movements easily brought her closer to climax. Each moment was more intense than the last. Her hands slid down, and she dug her fingers into Sally's butt, feeling her muscles clench with each thrust. Unwrapping her legs from around Sally's hips, Lucy placed her feet firmly on the seat of her chair as leverage to help her move closer against Sally. Thin garments separated flesh from warm and moist tissue and she delighted in the feel of her swollen need sliding against the cotton fabric of her panties. Lucy was forced to slow her movements in order to prolong her orgasm, trying her best not to explode too soon. She trailed her mouth down to Sally's neck and kissed her gently. Sally groaned and angled her head to the side, welcoming Lucy's lips and tongue to tease her playfully on her sensitive skin.

Despite her attempts at slowing the approaching climax, Lucy felt the continued tension build as the delicious pressure from Sally's groin became so intense that she burst into convulsions, causing her back to arch and her groin to thrust lustfully against her. As the convulsing peaked, Lucy dug her fingers into Sally's flesh, and she gently bit her shoulder to stop from yelling out in unadulterated ecstasy. Sally groaned and fell forward, her weight pushing Lucy backward. Sally's hips slowed but moved in a deeper intensity. They were almost entirely flat on her desk, her breathing becoming ragged and louder. Lucy was still pulsating when Sally cried out. By now, Lucy was flat on her back, giving Sally the space she needed for her orgasm. Sally's face slumped and dropped into the cusp of Lucy's shoulder, still breathing hard and groaning.

"Oh god," she whispered into Lucy's ear, her saliva wetting Lucy's skin as it cooled in the night air. She moved even deeper then, gripping Lucy's hips, pulling her tightly into her. Her weight pushed down on her as Lucy struggled for breath.

Lucy found her mouth again and kissed her as their orgasms started to fade. Sally returned her kisses passionately, eyes closed, perspiration trickling from her brow.

Lucy knew they would both be sporting slight bruising the following day, but that would be a reminder of just how raunchy this night had been.

This was what transpired on the third night of Lucy's seven nights' punishment, it continued each night thereafter.

†

The last night of Lucy's seven shifts turned out to be extraordinarily busy with fifteen new patients diagnosed with gastroenteritis. She just wanted to get home and drop into a soothing bath to wash off all invisible bacteria, and then settle down with a refreshingly cold beer. Thankfully it was the last day of her seven long shifts, so it meant she could look forward to a whole week off. The obliging night matron and Lucy had decided to keep their escapades just between the two of them, which suited Lucy just fine.

CHAPTER TWO

Lucy reached her house in Ramsgate within ten minutes after she left her last shift at the hospital. It was February and the South African summer heat never failed to disappoint with its excruciating humidity. As she walked in, she chucked her keys into the bowl at the entrance and lazily strode up to her fridge. The coolness of the air felt welcome on her skin as she opened the door. After she selected a cold beer, she slammed the fridge shut and opened the drink. Her laptop was on the dining room table. She sat herself down and took a long drink from the bottle before starting up the computer. While tapping her fingers impatiently on the tabletop, she made a mental note to sign into her email via her phone, so she could see any new incoming emails on her new iPhone. Generally, nurses were technologically disadvantaged, but her good friend, Paul, had given her countless hours in lessons on how to use it. Paul Curtis had been her best friend for many years and what made him so perfect was that he was a gay man. He never made her feel uncomfortable.

As the laptop buzzed into action, Lucy took another sip of her beer. There was only one email in her inbox when the screen came on, and it instantly made her stomach twist in tight knots. She felt her mouth turn dry, her palms sweat, and her throat constrict. Her heart knocked wildly with anxiety. The dreaded email was from her mother's email address. The only time she ever got mail from her mother was when something was terribly wrong. Her dad had already died, so she couldn't think of any other reason why she would receive an email from her. After downing half of her beer, she double-clicked on the message as if it were from Satan herself.

Dear Lucy,

My name is Cameron. I'm your mom's personal assistant. It is with great sadness and urgency that I am sending you this message. She's fallen ill and needs your assistance.

I have taken the liberty of booking you a flight. Details are attached. Please print the attachment, it has all the information. If you can't make it, kindly inform me so I can change your booking to a day that suits you better, but I don't think your mother has much time.

Regards,

Cameron Bishop.

Lucy had no idea how long she sat and stared at the email before she finally snapped back to reality. She opened the image and realized that the booking was for the following day. All her hopes of having a peaceful week off work evaporated. With shaky fingers, she took her phone from the table and dialed Paul's number.

"Finally. I thought your seven deathly sevens would never end. Missed you, Lucy." Paul's voice instantly quieted her nerves. He had the magic ability of calming any storm by just being there.

"Hey, Paulie. Me too. You have no idea. Worst week of my life. Well, except I finally seduced the all elusive Matron Smith." Lucy giggled.

"Lucy..." He over exaggerated a gasp. "You're such a slut."

"As if you aren't, Paulie," she teased, even though he had been in a committed relationship for many years.

"Hey, I've been very good since Alan and I decided to keep it monotonous."

"You mean monogamous," she corrected, but knew he'd used the word intentionally.

"That one," he said.

"I know. Well done."

"When are you ever going to settle down?"

"Paulie, you do *not* want to go there. That will never ever happen."

"Don't you get tired of your promiscuous existence?"

"Would you?"

"You have a point." He laughed.

"Anyway, you know we've had this talk before. Countless times. Best you let it be."

"So, want to meet for a drink this evening? Alan has a theatre list as long as my shlong. He won't be home till very late."

Lucy chuckled. "That's a picture I most definitely don't want on my mind. Drinks? Great idea. What time?"

"You just worked all night. Sleep a few hours and meet me at Man Cave at five."

"Nice try. You will never get me to Man Cave, tiger. How about we meet at Pistols instead?"

"Five. Not a minute after."

"Sure."

After Lucy ended the call, she emptied the last of her beer, took the bath she had been looking forward to and fell into bed. The last thought that clouded her mind before drifting off was of her past.

†

"Hey, girlfriend." Paul hated it when anyone called him that, but Lucy loved teasing him. She placed her arms around his neck in a friendly hug.

He was seated on a stool at the bar, chatting to the young bartender when she had arrived. "Juicy Lucy." He returned her hug affectionately.

The bartender frowned at their warm display but didn't say anything.

Paul winked at him. "Lucy and I have been friends for years."

The bartender nodded, his face expressionless.

"We met in nursing college," he said before looking at her again. "What's your poison, honey bun? Beer?"

"Beer sounds great." She sighed as she shrugged her backpack off her shoulder and dropped it to the floor before taking the seat next to him.

The barman placed the cold beer in front of her. "Can I get you a glass?" he asked as he wiped a spot that was invisible to the naked eye.

"No, thanks." She raised the bottle. "It's already in a glass."

"Sure," he said before turning his attention to another customer.

"How's Alan?" Lucy asked as she took a sip and glanced over at Paul.

"My hubby is doing great. His practice is super busy right now. Every woman in town wants a boob job."

"I'm sure your plastic surgeon husband knows more about breasts than I do."

Paul laughed. "I very much doubt that."

"How are things at home, Paulie? I noticed you flirting a bit with the gorgeous bartender."

"Things are going great. I wasn't flirting, don't stress." He patted her arm for a second.

"Good to hear, you're the cutest couple I know."

"Alan freaked when I told him I'm meeting you for drinks. He warned me that I'd better be sober when he gets home. And you know how macho he is, even with his tight butt and all." Paul flipped his wrist and placed his hand on his cheek at the mention of how manly Alan was.

"Oh, Paulie, even Alan at his most masculine is far more feminine than most females." Lucy shook her head before taking a sip of her beer. It always amazed her how much in love the two men were with each other. She cleared her throat before she spoke again. "I got a very unexpected email today. Apparently, my mother's ill. She allegedly needs me at home. My plane leaves tomorrow."

Paul's eyes grew wide as Lucy spoke the words. His hand still stuck to his cheek, fifth digital slightly raised. "Oh my god, Looce. You're going?" Paul and Alan were the only people who knew of Lucy's parents and her past, and she preferred it that way. Her personal life was kept locked away, for no one to see.

"Her PA emailed me an eTicket."

"And you're going?" His eyes were still wide.

"I have to go, Paulie. I don't know why, but something inside me is telling me I must do this. Maybe for closure."

"Of course. I understand. Are you all right, though?" He placed his hand on hers, his tone soft. "And when will you be back?" Paul had the gentlest of voices.

"I'm fine, I guess. And I'll be back once the old hag crosses over."

"I'm so sorry, sweetie. I don't know what else to say."

"It's okay. This was about to happen sooner or later. I guess it's time to face my demons." She downed the rest of her beer and as she signaled for the bartender to bring them a refill, Paul spoke.

"It must be so hard for you. If they were my parents, I'd never be able to return."

"It's such a shock to me too, Paulie. It's been so long since I heard from either of them. I was sixteen. It was what," Lucy counted off on her fingers, "fifteen years ago."

"Fifteen years or a hundred. It doesn't matter. What they did to you was unforgivable." Paul shivered.

The bartender placed two more drinks in front of them.

"Thanks," Lucy said and immediately drank from hers. "What doesn't kill you makes you stronger. Besides, I'm not that frightened little girl I once was."

"Do you still have all that money your dad gave you?"

"It's been invested. I don't need their goddamned money. I can fend for myself." Remembering how her dad

19

did his *fatherly duties* by transferring a million Rand into her bank account after he'd sent her packing made her blood boil all over again. He literally paid her to stay out of their lives.

Paul reached out and placed his soft hand on her arm. "I know. You're one of the strongest people I know." His blue eyes were soft and tender when he spoke.

"It sickens me to think they thought they could buy me off."

Paul shook his head. "Instead of being defeated, you went straight to nursing school. Did something important with your life."

"Yeah. Never spent so much as a cent of their money." Lucy gritted her teeth, trying to bite back the anger.

"I still can't believe the way he ordered you to stop contacting them." He raised his glass. "Here's a toast to you, the warrior."

Lucy raised her beer bottle and gently touched his glass. "Cheers."

After sipping from his drink, he put it down on the counter and played with the condensation that had made a little puddle under his glass. "He made his millions selling water, calling it... what did he call it again...?" Paul's voice drifted off.

"Holy healing water."

Paul snapped his fingers. "That's the one. So many people fell for his scam. Bought tap water believing it would heal them."

Lucy grimaced. "He made billions off of his gullible followers."

"Your fake healer dad became one of the most beloved celebrities in the world."

"He was basically the leader of a cult with millions of followers." She grinned at Paul. "My dad was an asshole."

"Yup, no one saw through his farce."

"Little did they know what was happening behind the scenes. Like, who would believe that a 'holy man's' daughter could be pregnant at sixteen." Lucy swallowed the lump in her throat.

Paul gently touched her arm. "I'm always here for you, Lucy."

"He told the tabloids that I had drowned. That brought him even more fame and sympathy from his fans." Her heart clenched at the memory of seeing that information by accident when one of her patients was watching TV while she was at their bedside. "Will you take me to the airport tomorrow, please, Paulie?"

"Of course, sweetie. That's what friends are for." Paul flicked his left wrist as he spoke, and then he leaned forward and murmured, "You know how I love the cabin crew."

She slapped him on his arm. "Behave."

†

Paul picked her up at nine am, even though her flight was booked for twelve. He loved airports, and always said that the cabin crew gave him fever. Cabin fever. The airport was busy as usual. It took Lucy half an hour before she finally got the assistance she needed at the flight desk. Paul waited for her at the vending machine, talking to a little girl of about four, who was skipping around happily. Lucy thought about what a great dad he would make one day and smiled. She turned her attention back to the counter when it was finally her turn to book in. The pretty face that bobbed up from behind the counter took notice of her immediately. She blushed when her fingers touched Lucy's hand as she reached for the one-way ticket to hell. Lucy's flirting instinct kicked in automatically, so she returned her smile, placed her elbows on the counter, and leaned forward onto her desk.

"What's your name, beautiful?" Lucy asked.

"Candy." While tapping the info into her computer, she continued to blush. "I have a break in a half hour, and your flight doesn't leave for another two. Want to go for a drink or something?"

Or something. Tempting. Lucy glanced over at Paul, who glared back at her with a warning. She sighed and turned her attention back to Candy. "No, I don't think that's a good idea. I'm here with a friend. But thanks for the invite. Maybe when I get back?"

Candy's smile vanished, and she focused on her computer screen for a moment before inhaling sharply. "One way ticket."

After her luggage was booked in, she returned to Paul. "I see you made a new friend. I haven't even left yet and you're already replacing me." She teased him, referring to the little girl he had been talking to.

"I'm not replacing you. I'm just upgrading. My new friend is way more mature than you." He smiled sincerely at her, took her hand, and led her to the bar closest to the boarding gates.

"Two beers, please," Paul ordered and paid for the drinks.

They chose seats by the window, so they could watch the planes land. He leaned over the table to take hold of her hands and held onto them. "How am I going to cope without you, baby girl?"

She smiled at him but had to swallow before she spoke. The lump in her throat had made it difficult to breathe. "Same here. Who's going to go clothing shopping with me? And worse, who is going to help me dress appropriately for each occasion?"

"Hell, girl. What *are* you going to wear while in Cape Town without my expertise? Please always remember to wear the black belt with those black boots of yours, and don't combine bright colors with—"

"Chill, girlfriend," Lucy interjected. "I don't plan on going out, so I'm sure I'll be fine. I packed my scrubs, which is what I plan on wearing anyway." She was only kidding, but Paul became undone. Years of nursing had taught her how to deal with hysterical patients, and this skill she often used on Paul. "I'm just pulling your leg, Paul. Calm your willy."

They sat and talked until it was time for her to board the plane, and nothing could have prepared her for the weeping that was awaiting her. Paul sobbed like a baby, as if she would never return. He held onto her, while wetting her shoulder. "Shhh shhh shhh…" Lucy comforted him, patting him on the back of his head. She wanted to join him in the crying, but knew she had to be strong for him. *It's always worse for the people that are left behind.*

Her shoulder was drenched when she eventually took her seat on the plane, and then she could finally let go of her own tears. She cried secretly for about a minute before liftoff. Once they were airborne, she ordered a drink and sipped it slowly. She needed to be numb enough for the trip. And more importantly, she had to get her mind on track. She hadn't seen her mother in fifteen years, and she wasn't nearly ready for this mother-daughter reunion just yet.

CHAPTER THREE

Getting off the plane in Cape Town two hours later made her feel like running away and never looking back again, but she knew she had to face her fears. Of course, her mother wasn't there to collect her. She'd already known that but couldn't help scanning the crowd for her mom's face. Lucy wondered what she looked like now after all this time. When she didn't find anyone familiar in the crowd of expectant faces, she couldn't help but envy the majority of people who were greeted happily with hugs and smiles. Lucy then scanned through the name boards for her name, and it didn't take her long to find the one that read "Lucy Donald".

The person who held the iPad with her name on it immediately caught Lucy's eye. She was a very attractive, tall woman with long brown hair that cascaded down her shoulders in soft curls. Her serious eyes looked somber. The two-piece custom-tailored pantsuit she wore revealed long slender legs, and she had a confident posture that commanded attention. Everything about her exuded an air of sophistication and poise that one couldn't simply ignore. As she remained still in the crowd, her presence seemed to draw gazes from both men and women alike. Lucy took a deep breath and walked up to her, and as she neared, she noticed her bright blue eyes expressed a variety of emotions. Lucy nodded at her.

Her expression looked forced. "Lucy?"

"That's me," Lucy confirmed and tried to smile up at her, but she was sure it didn't reach her eyes. Her heart pounded in her ears, and she had to stop herself from turning around and booking a flight back home.

As she tucked the iPad under her arm, the woman said, "This way to the car." She then turned and marched off.

With a backpack slung over Lucy's left shoulder, a suitcase dragging behind her on its wonky wheels, and a sense of urgency in her heart, she embarked on a hurried walk, trying to keep up. Lucy's mind raced with a thousand thoughts. Exchanges of fleeting glances and muffled conversations blurred together, as if the world around her moved in fast forward. But amidst the hurried chaos, Lucy couldn't help but notice the snippets of life that unfolded around her. A laughter-filled conversation, a couple sharing a tender moment, a child skipping alongside a parent. She realized that even in the midst of her rushed journey, there was a whole world moving at its own pace, each person living their own narrative. It was a reminder to find balance amidst the hustle.

Of course, the car was a limo. Lucy froze when they reached their destination. She wasn't used to this lifestyle anymore, so she looked around self-consciously, hoping that no one would notice her when she clambered in. She recognized the driver immediately. Olaf was the same driver her parents had when she grew up.

"Ms. Lucy." He looked ecstatic to see her.

"Olaf, nice to see you again." She suddenly felt a bit calmer at being recognized by the chauffeur she had known and loved so many years ago. It was good to see a familiar, friendly face. No thanks to the cold shoulder she had run into upon arrival.

Olaf took her luggage, and after she got in, closed the door for her.

The tall woman walked around to the other side and got in diagonally across from her. She smoothed out her pants and jacket, making sure they didn't crease on the long drive home.

"Are you Cameron?" Lucy spoke politely, hoping that they could become friends instead of enemies. If she was about to survive this visit, she was hell bound on making it as pleasant as she possibly could. It was second nature for her to be polite, as that was what she was taught in nursing college.

"Correct." Cameron was quite obviously unhappy with Lucy's arrival, and Lucy wondered why Cameron had even bothered sending her the email when she could have easily just lied to her mother.

The scent of fresh leather filled the spacious interior, setting the tone for an unforgettable journey. Olaf gave a polite nod, and with a gentle press on the accelerator, the limousine glided smoothly onto the open road.

The smooth ride, coupled with the tinted windows, created a sense of privacy and luxury. As she settled into the plush leather seats, Lucy found herself captivated by the passing scenery. Tall buildings and bustling city streets gradually gave way to a more serene landscape as the limousine took them out of the city.

The gentle hum of the engine provided a soothing background noise, almost like a lullaby. The trip felt effortless, and she relished the opportunity to fully relax and let the world outside melt away.

The limousine continued along a scenic route, passing by rolling hills, peaceful lakes, and idyllic countryside. The sunlight filtered through the windows, casting warm rays onto her face, creating a tranquil ambiance within the vehicle.

Lucy tore her eyes from the beautiful scene of nature outside the vehicle and glanced at Cameron's serious face. "Tell me about Angela."

Cameron paused for a moment, and then sighed before she spoke. "She has a brain tumor and is bedridden, but being the stubborn lady that she is, she refuses to have any nurse take care of her, and she insisted I ask you to come and look after her. Don't worry too much…" She swallowed and continued, "I don't think she has too long left." Her expression turned cold as ice when she added, "And then you can get back to whatever it is you do with your life. You will of course be compensated for your valuable time 'wasted' here."

Her cold attitude grieved Lucy to the chore. "Great. I don't want to stay here long. I'll just stick around for a while and try to figure out what it is that she really wants, and then I'll be out of your hair, and leave you to it." She felt irritated with Cameron's unnecessary annoyance with her when she had no reason to be rude. Cameron didn't even know her. "What are you to her anyway?" Lucy asked, curious to know if she was sticking around for some other inheritance. Lucy wanted nothing from her mother. If she needed money, she would work for it. She wasn't interested in any handouts.

"I'm her personal assistant, as per my email." Cameron turned her attention to the trees outside.

Lucy rolled her eyes. As if she couldn't figure that out for herself. That was not what she had meant. She knew she was her PA for heaven's sake. She really wanted to know what her involvement was with the estate. And with her mother. After a long moment of uncomfortable silence, Lucy attempted again at making conversation. If they were going to spend some time together while Lucy cared for her mother, she wanted them to at least try being friends. Lucy reached over, touched her arm and leaned closer. "Are you from Britain? I like your accent."

Cameron's eyes shot to Lucy's hand on her arm. "Obviously." Then she turned her gaze back to the road.

Lucy let her hand drop. "Quite the chatterbox, aren't you?"

She continued with her silence, staring off into the distance.

Five minutes later. "If you insist on talking nonstop like this, I can't guarantee that I'll be listening to you for much longer." A few minutes later she continued. "Please can you keep quiet for a while? My ears are ringing already."

Her lips twitched slightly, but before they managed to form a smile, Cameron glanced at her. "We're here."

That's when Lucy noticed the limo had stopped in front of her old house. Cameron got out, and took off without another word, leaving Lucy on her own.

Olaf nodded at Lucy and smiled broadly. "I'll put your luggage in your room, Ms. Lucy."

"Thanks, Olaf." She was grateful for his cheer. She would need a friendly face by the look of things. He appeared to be in his sixties by now, but he had aged well. He was still very attractive with his dark hair that had greyed just above his ears.

Lucy gaped at the magnificent palace her old house had become. It was three times the size it used to be and had changed a lot since she had been there. Her heart raced in her chest as she sauntered up to the door. A man stood in the doorway, looking at her with patience in his eyes.

"Ms. Lucy, I'm Robert, the butler. I'm very pleased to finally meet you." Robert, a medium built gentleman with short blond hair, impeccably dressed, stuck his hand out at her as she entered the front door.

She took his outstretched gloved hand and shook it. "Obliged," she said, wondering if that was the correct word. She wasn't used to these formalities anymore and felt more than slightly out of place.

"Would you like a tour?" he offered.

"I think that might be needed, otherwise I'm going to get lost."

He bowed his head and led the way, starting the tour of the entire fifteen-acre estate.

As they stepped into the enchanting garden, an array of vibrant colors, fragrant flowers, and lush greenery surrounded them. The air carried the sweet scent of blooming blossoms, rejuvenating Lucy's senses and drawing her deeper into the natural wonderland. It wasn't long before they reached the pool.

"How many bedrooms are there now, Robert?" Lucy asked as they strolled around the Olympic-sized swimming pool.

"The main residence has ten bedrooms, and then there are a few guest houses on the plot too, for the staff." He pointed to the cottages that could barely be seen in the distance.

She followed him past the pool, which had a fully stocked bar, and admired the perennial gardens. The pathways, adorned with delicate pebbles and meandering around manicured lawns, invited Lucy to embark on a leisurely stroll. She followed the winding trail, taking her time to appreciate the intricacy of the garden's design and the harmonious symphony of scents that permeated the air.

Quite a distance past the pool area, the ground gave way. About thirty yards below she could see the ocean and waves crashing against large, black rocks. Lucy leaned as far as she could so she could see to the bottom of the cliff. "Wow. I've forgotten how beautiful it is here." The wind whipped her hair and she shivered. The Western Cape was slightly colder than Ramsgate. A chill ran up her spine, but the fresh air was very welcoming.

"Careful. Don't get too close to the edge, Miss."

She felt the slight touch of Robert's gentle hand on her shoulder and took a big step back.

He smiled. "There's more. Come."

As they ambled along, they came across a variety of flowers. Roses, in countless hues, showcasing their velvety petals, exuded elegance and grace. The soft whisper of a gentle breeze caused the blooms to sway delicately, their fragrance intensifying with each passing gust.

Farther along the path, they encountered a tranquil pond, its surface calm and reflective like a mirror. Koi fish glided effortlessly through the water, their vibrant colors captivating Lucy's attention. Nearby, a quaint wooden bench invited her to sit and immerse herself in the serenity of the surroundings.

The garden's meticulously arranged plants and foliage created a sense of harmony and balance. Towering trees provided shade, their branches reaching upward as if trying to embrace the heavens. As sunlight filtered through the leaves, it created a mesmerizing play of light and shadow, painting the garden in an ever-changing canvas of beauty.

Each step she took revealed new delights, from tall hedges forming lush natural walls to delicate arbors adorned with climbing vines. Birds sang their melodious tunes, adding a symphony of sounds that blended seamlessly with the garden's tranquility.

As they continued their stroll, they came across hidden nooks and secret corners, inviting Lucy to explore and lose herself in their charm. She paused occasionally to touch velvety petals, feeling their softness under her fingertips, and to take in the breathtaking vistas that unfolded before her.

Throughout their meandering journey, time seemed to slow down, allowing Lucy to fully savor every moment in this blissful sanctuary. As they reached the end of their stroll, Lucy carried with her a sense of peace, rejuvenation, and an overwhelming appreciation for the delicate yet powerful beauty of nature.

Robert finally turned and headed back to the house. Lucy followed him eagerly, curious to see what awaited her within the majestic walls of her old home. On the way back they passed a beautiful gazebo. The thatched-roof gazebo was covered in fairy lights and there was a massive fountain in the middle. By the time they reached the house Lucy was slightly out of breath. As they entered the foyer, she gasped at the changes that had taken place since she had last set foot there. Robert was talking, but she wasn't listening to his ramblings about how the place had been built and which architects had been involved with which parts of the structure. That part didn't interest her in the least, but she was impressed by his knowledge.

The living room opened to a covered veranda. The formal dining room had a hidden bar which, as Robert demonstrated, one could access with just the touch of a button. She could easily get lost in the house, or rather, the mansion.

The family room had a magnificent marble fireplace. Robert led her down a long passage. Her father's office was at the end of the passage, right after the staircase that led to the bedrooms on the first and second floors. He showed Lucy her mother's room, which was on the ground floor, right opposite the stairway. Lucy hesitated for a second, but she didn't go in. Robert then led the way upstairs to the second floor. He stopped in front of a closed bedroom door. "These are your living quarters, Miss."

"Thank you, Robert. That was quite the tour."

"No problem, Miss." He bowed his head before he walked off.

Her room was almost an exact replica of her old room. It wasn't the same one, seeing as the old house must have been demolished almost entirely, but someone had put in great effort in trying to recreate the space as it used to be. Even all her old posters had been stuck to the walls. She opened her closet doors and gasped when she saw all her old clothes hanging on the railing. As she carefully ran her fingers over the fabric, a wave of mixed emotions washed over her. The worn and weathered textures told a story of the countless moments these garments had witnessed, the memories they held, and the lives they had adorned.

Each piece carried a unique history, as evidenced by the frayed edges, faded colors, and well-worn seams. Lucy could almost feel the passage of time beneath her fingertips, as if the fabric itself held the echoes of bygone eras.

The touch of her old clothes was ineffably evocative. As Lucy explored the material, her mind wandered, remembering the life she had once lived.

Each fabric had its own unique feel, evoking different emotions and reminiscences. The scent of her old clothes mingled with her touch, triggering a flood of memories. The aroma transported her back to her childhood, family gatherings, a time in her life that she had long tried to forget. It was as if the fabrics held onto the essence of the past, leaving Lucy with feelings of angst that pinched at her stomach.

She didn't have the strength to go back down to her mother's room, as it was five pm and she desperately needed some rest. Seven nights of night duty was not a great immunization against her mother's monstrous charms, so she took a quick shower before she jumped onto her bed. She dug in her bag and found the big packet of crisps and the can of orange juice she had packed the night before. Lucy got comfortable and ate and drank while chatting to Paul via text, telling him about her safe arrival and the inauspicious PA who had collected her from the airport.

†

Lucy slept like the dead and when she finally awoke it was ten am. Feeling slightly ashamed, she ran through the shower and dressed in jeans and a black tank top. Before she left her room, she peeked at her reflection in the mirror. For someone who had just slept twelve hours straight, she looked awful. Her blue eyes were surrounded by a red lining, and her skin looked pale. She brushed her fingers through her hair before she dared leaving her room. Any excuse would do, as long as she didn't have to face her mother immediately, so she scampered down the two flights of stairs toward the kitchen. A strong cup of coffee would have to do the trick in place of the breakfast she had obviously missed.

Unfortunately, coffee would have to be accompanied by the unfriendly face of Cameron Bishop, because when Lucy finally set foot in the kitchen, the PA was slumped in a chair by the kitchen table. Cameron looked worse for wear and Lucy couldn't help but wonder what could be causing her to look so utterly defeated.

Knowing what a blabber mouth she was, *not*, Lucy ignored her negative aura, and poured herself a cup of coffee. She heard Cameron clearing her throat behind her, so Lucy reluctantly turned to face her.

"Have you gone to see her yet?"

Wow, it speaks.

Cameron's eyes were sad, and she looked like she hadn't slept a wink. Lucy hated it when people were upset, so her immediate instinct was to be nice. She didn't know what to say or how to act in order to comfort her, suspecting the PA hated her for absolutely no reason. Instead, Lucy decided to overlook her gloom.

"Going in a minute," she mumbled before taking a sip of her coffee.

"Not very enthusiastic. What type of a daughter are you?"

"The kind that doesn't want to be here." Lucy swallowed.

"You haven't seen her in *years*, and even though you've been here almost a whole day, you haven't even bothered. What made you so cruel? Your poor mother."

Anger made her hands tremble as she attempted at another sip of her coffee. It infuriated her when people made assumptions, and Cameron had no idea what type of person Lucy was. Hell, Lucy hardly knew herself, how dare she insinuate that s*he* did? She mulled it over for a while, and decided not to get into an argument, so she slammed her coffee mug down, turned around and left. It was time anyway, and she desperately needed to get it over with.

The passage swam around her on the way to her mother's bedroom, and when she reached her mother's door, she froze before entering, taking a moment to catch her breath. The bedroom was still exactly how Lucy remembered it, except for the fireplace which was new. They must have built this new mansion around parts of the old house. She noticed it was one of those fancy gas fireplaces which went all the way through to the bathroom. The thick woven beige carpets were so soft that Lucy's shoes felt as if they sank three inches with her weight as she entered the room.

Her mother looked weak and frail as she lay there in her bed with the IV and the oxygen generating machines that surrounded her. Even at the sight of her, Lucy struggled to find any sympathy from within herself. This was the woman who had ripped her heart out and stepped onto it in gravel. Lucy hated her. With all her heart. Whatever Lucy had felt for her so long ago was wiped away together with the oceans of tears she had cried over the years. All those lonely nights she had cried herself to sleep took care of any remaining emotions equivalent to love. There was nothing left. Nothing but pity and hatred for the sixty-year-old stranger, who was shrinking away in her bed. To think how afraid she used to be of her and look at her now. She was fading away. Lucy inched closer to her bed and looked down at her. Her grey hair had started thinning, her eyes were tired and weary. She was wrapped in a soft blanket, as if seeking comfort and relief from the pain.

"Claire?" She uttered weakly, fiddling with her oxygen mask. Her movements slow and measured.

"No, it's me. Lucy." She sighed. She had never imagined that her mother could look like this. She was always as hard as a cardboard box, but now she looked withered and emaciated. And that only at sixty. She looked eighty.

"What in the name of..." Angela breathed slowly, her chest sounding wheezy. "Lucy?" Her feeble voice had a slight pitch to it, aggravated by the wheezing. "How... ?" The lines of worry evident on her face spoke, due to the pain and struggle she must have endured on a daily basis.

39

"Not for the reasons you might think, Angela. I don't need your lousy fucking money. Don't worry. I'm leaving now anyway." As Lucy wanted to leave, Angela's iced bony fingers gripped her arm. Make no mistake, the shrunken old woman still had a grip like steel. Lucy flinched away from her grip, but her mother held on like a vice. The pathetic little child inside of Lucy needed to hear what the witch had to say, subconsciously hoping it would be something sweet, the way mothers were supposed to be.

"Stay," she muttered into her oxygen mask.

After years of rejection and resentment, why now all of a sudden? With that last thought, Lucy pulled her arm free and left.

Lucy returned to the kitchen, where Cameron was still slouched where she had left her a few moments ago. She looked like she was carrying the world on her shoulders, and it was weighing her down. Her brow was furrowed, with a downward curve to her lips.

Lucy was furious with her. She had lied to her, telling her that her mother had wanted her there. Angry at herself for believing that after all these years her mom could finally accept her and love her the way a mom was supposed to. "You lied. My mother never asked me to come, did she?" Lucy could see that she had caught Cameron by surprise, and her sullen eyes shot up at the harshness of Lucy's spoken words, and she was immediately on the defensive. "Why the heck did you bring me all the way over here?"

"What are you talking about?" Cameron had a sense of detachment in her demeanor.

"I am referring to the fact that she had no idea I was coming," Lucy grumbled. She didn't recognize her own voice as the anger bubbled over her lips.

"Your mother has a brain tumor. I believe you should at least give me the benefit of the doubt. Half the time she has no idea what she's saying."

"Why am I really here?" Lucy walked over to where Cameron sat and leaned over her. Their faces were only inches apart, and she could feel her breath on her face. Her breathing was uneven, and she must have thought that Lucy was going to kiss her, as her gaze fell to Lucy's lips. She looked uncomfortable, so Lucy moved away slightly.

"I think I know what you're trying to do." Lucy looked her straight in the eyes and refused to break eye contact. "Surely my mother doesn't need a personal assistant anymore, and you know that. She has enough servants to keep her company." Her words were laced with anger, as she felt the fire of rage burn inside her.

"Does it not even occur to you that maybe I care about her? You mother is a beautiful, caring person and does not deserve a brat like you as an only child."

That last comment sliced through her like a knife. Lucy took a step back but kept eye contact. "I know you're after the inheritance." She bit her lip, instantly regretting her

41

retort, backed away from Cameron, and sat down in a chair across from her.

"You don't know me, and you have no right to accuse me of any such things." Cameron breathed hard. Lucy could see the anger taking over her usually charming cold self.

"I bet my mother is paying you an astronomical salary for living here free of charge. You're just riding this one out right until the very end, aren't you?" That was a rhetorical question. Cameron had no need to respond, yet she tried.

"W—"

"I can see right through people like you," Lucy interjected. "Taking advantage of the terminally ill, like a hyena pouncing for the money hill. Oh, and don't worry, your secret is safe with me. I don't want anything from her. You can have it all." Lucy inspected her face as she spoke. "On one condition."

Her blue eyes were blazing hot, and she was breathing very hard. But she didn't say a word, so Lucy placed her condition on the table for her to ogle over. She loved the power she had over women, and this one was no different.

"Sleep with me."

"Fuck you." Cameron shoved her chair back so hard, that the side of it hit the table, sending her coffee flying down, the mug landing on the floor with a loud crash. Without giving Lucy one more look, she hurriedly left the kitchen.

Lucy frowned at herself and at her own outburst. It was not like her to harass women like that, and she had no interest in sleeping with Cameron, because a one-sided affair held no appeal for her, but she would enjoy toying with Cameron, knowing she was just after her family's money.

†

That evening, Lucy called the hospital and spoke to the matron.

"Hey, Sally. How's it going?"

"Lucy. Good to hear from you. I'm well, but quit the small talk. What can I do for you?"

"My mom's very ill and I need to spend some time with her. I need a month or so, please. Last time I checked I had six weeks annual leave owed to me. I'd like to take some of it."

"Sure, I'll let HR know."

"Thanks."

"Are you okay?" Her voice was filled with concern.

"I'm fine. I just really need to be here."

"Sure, no problem. Let me know if you need anything."

"Thanks," Lucy said. It was good hearing her voice.

"Oh, and Lucy?"

"Yes?"

"Take the full six weeks. Let me know if you need more, we can always make a plan."

43

"If I need more, I'll let you know. Thanks."

Six weeks meant twelve weeks, because Lucy worked one week on and had one week off. She sighed at the thought of spending twelve weeks away from Paul. She just had the sense that something was wrong and needed to be here. Even though she hated her mother, she was her only living family.

†

The following morning was a beautiful, warm day and Lucy decided to take a quick run within the grounds. The property was big enough for her to get some steps in, along all the little trails, and she wanted to make the most of her stay and enjoy the beautiful gardens, with the koi pond and fountains. It was upon passing the swimming pool that Lucy spotted the stranger. She was in a two-piece bathing suit, and her body was perfect. Her long blond hair was wet, sleeked back against her head. She lay on a deck chair, with her face turned upward. Lucy's eyes followed her perfect shape downward, her breasts were firm, and her nipples erect from the cool water. Her stomach was completely flat, and she had a tattoo of a dragon on her hip. She suddenly turned her face in Lucy's direction.

Lucy switched direction and headed for the pool. "How's the water?" she asked, trying to control her breathing. She had run quite a distance.

The blonde said nothing and glanced at Lucy with an annoyed expression. She sat up and reached for her iced tea.

What a 'friendly' bunch. Lucy walked to the pool, kneeled over and dipped her hand into the cool water. It felt great. She straightened, flipped off her running shoes, removed her top as well as her sports bra, then her shorts, only leaving her silky panties on. She glanced back at the woman, smiled, and dove into the pool. When Lucy came up for air, the woman stood by the far end of the pool, watching her intensely.

"Join me," Lucy flirted with a wink.

"You really should put a swimsuit on. You know, there are gardeners on the grounds."

Lucy swam to where she stood, and crossed her arms over the side, leaning her chin on top of her hands. "I will if you join me," she answered.

"No thanks," she said and walked back to her seat.

Lucy lifted herself from the pool and walked over to the woman. "And who might you be?"

"Just leaving," she muttered as she gathered her towel, and walked off.

†

Lucy heard hushed voices talking when she passed her mother's room on the way to the stairwell, so she stopped by the door and listened.

"Lucy?" her mother's frail voice called from within the bedroom.

How the hell did she know I was here? Did her voodoo doll inform her? Lucy walked in, and saw Cameron sitting next to her, holding her hand. "Yes, Angela. It's me, Lucy. The daughter you banished." She regretted the words as soon as they were out.

"Come here." Her breathing was loud and wheezy. Her voice muffled by the oxygen mask that covered her face.

As a daughter was supposed to do, and curious as to what she was going to say, Lucy obeyed and walked closer. Her mother's grey hair was spread all over her pillows, her eyes blown red by the continuous oxygen. "What's up?" Lucy asked.

"Please... My back is killing me..."

"Will you help me turn her?" Cameron looked hopeful as she spoke. "Claire and Gwen usually assist with this, but they're busy helping Connie in the kitchen."

Angela's king-sized bed had been replaced with an electronic hospital bed, one of those technologically advanced, remote-controlled ones that practically required a degree to operate. Lucy went to the opposite side of the bed and took her mother's bony shoulder in order to turn her onto her side, while Cameron placed some pillows as support behind her, to keep her from flopping back down onto her back. Then, with expert movements, Lucy placed a pillow between her knees and pulled the cot-side up, so that she wouldn't fall off the bed. She returned to the other side, where Cameron was trying to balance her mother so she wouldn't fall back down, and said, "I got this."

Cameron stepped aside and watched Lucy as she rubbed some lotion onto her mom's back.

"You see how red her back is? This is from lying in the same position for too long. If she gets bedsores, she could get septicemia."

"No wonder she was complaining of pain." Cameron's eyes looked sad as she spoke.

"Has she eaten yet?"

"She had a few bites," Cameron said while she stroked Angela's hair.

"I'm famished. Do you think I could score some food?"

"Connie, the cook, will have made lunch by now. She usually sets up in the dining room."

"Oh my. I remember Connie. Can't believe she's still here."

"Been here since I started working for your mom."

"Care to join me?" She looked over at Cameron who smiled gently.

"Sure," she said. Her moods were such a roller coaster. Lucy never knew what to expect from her.

Cameron led the way to the dining room. Lucy sat and marveled at the spread in front of her. Connie had prepared an exquisite cuisine. Each dish was a work of art, succeeding at enticing all Lucy's senses and transporting her to a realm of pure gastronomic delight. The air was filled with tantalizing aromas. A perfectly succulent, slow-roasted lamb, infused with rosemary and garlic, accompanied by sugar snap peas and tender asparagus. The meat looked juicy and tender, and the presentation simply stunning. There was so much food that it made her feel guilty, thinking about people starving all over the country. She dished until her plate was full and started eating. Her eyes wandered over to Cameron. She couldn't help but admire the way she moved while she dished food onto her plate, picked up her fork, and neatly gathered a bite before placing it into her mouth.

Cameron swallowed and observed Lucy for a moment. "Are you going to stay?"

"You really should chew your food, you know," Lucy said as she watched her take another bite. "I hate bad nursing care, so yes. I'll stay to look after her."

Cameron sighed and looked somewhat relieved. "Thank you."

"But then you have to help me when I need help. I'm not doing this alone. Do we have a deal?"

"Does this include sexual favors?"

Lucy laughed. "That deal is off the table. You had your chance and blew it."

That's the first time she noticed Cameron had dimples in her cheeks, as her lips curved upward. "Your loss."

"I'm genuinely sorry about that. Since my arrival, you've been giving me the cold shoulder. I guess I was just trying to intimidate you."

"Apology accepted." Cameron cleared her throat and continued, "Claire and Gwen help feed and wash your mother. I just need your help teaching them enough so that your mother gets all the right care she needs. I don't want her to get any pressure ulcers, and I don't want her to be in any pain. She has morphine syrup, which we've been giving her, but I think you should take over that responsibility, seeing as you're medically qualified."

"Of course. I understand," Lucy agreed. She took a bite of vegetables and chewed. After she swallowed, she continued, "You were good with her in there. She's lucky to have you."

"From what I can see, you guys had some or other falling out that I don't know the full story of, but you should try and give her a chance. She has been calling for you for quite some time."

Lucy bit back a negative retort. "I'm not comfortable discussing the past with you," was all she said.

"Noted," Cameron said as she finished off the last of her food.

"You really ought to chew, Cameron," Lucy said with a hint of humor in her voice.

Cameron ignored her mocking. "I'll help you with everything you need to do for your mom. I promise. I'm glad you decided to stay."

After they finished their lunch, they parted ways for the rest of the day.

†

That night, back in her room, Lucy's phone rang. It was Paul. She smiled and answered, "Hello, your majesty." *Isn't that how you addressed the queen after all?*

"Ooh, girlfriend, guess where we're going?"

"Uhm, I give up. Spill."

"Paris!" He pronounced it "Parree." Lucy had to move the phone ten inches away from her ear, or else he would have blasted her eardrum.

"What the hell are you going to do there, Paulie?"

"Make babies." A high-pitched giggle. Phone farther away from her ear.

"Uh, did you and I go to the same nursing school?"

"We can at least try, can't we?" A squeal. Ouch.

Lucy put her phone on speaker mode and placed it on the bed. "That's so exciting, Paulie. When are you leaving?"

"This weekend, and we'll be gone for three weeks!" He sounded so excited, that Lucy could imagine him jumping up and down, popcorn style. She was happy for him, but he was her only support system. She knew she wouldn't be able to call him three times a day if he was prancing around in Paris, he needed some quality time with Alan.

"That's fabulous. I'm super-duper jealous."

"I wish you could come with. How's your mom, by the way?"

"She's sick as fuck, Paulie. But please don't worry about me. Go have a wonderful time."

"How long will you be staying there, Juicy Lucy?"

"I don't know. Probably a few weeks. I put in leave, so I can relax and figure out my next step without stressing about work, at least."

"See? It helps to sleep with the boss, doesn't it?"

"Right, you would know."

"Alan is the best thing that could ever have happened to me. I am so happy, Lucy. I wish you could also meet your lid even though you're a bit of a cracked pot." He giggled. "You know I'm only joking, right? Someone will be lucky to have you."

"Yeah, I know. But you and me both know I'm not marriage material."

"Snot. You'll meet the right person. You'll see."

After a few more minutes of chatting, they ended the call, and for a moment Lucy wished she could also be head over heels in love with just one special person. The moment didn't last long, however. She had never been in love before. Up until now, she had thrived in a world of independence and adventure. Her days were filled with spontaneity and endless possibilities, as she immersed herself in new experiences and short, meaningless relationships. Lucy had always been drawn to the energy and excitement of the unknown. Relationships, to her, felt like heavy chains that would bind her spirit, taking away the freedom she cherished so dearly. She loved the thrill of uncertainty, the exhilaration of spontaneity. But deep down, a part of her longed for something more, a connection that went beyond fleeting encounters. Why would that ever change? She had contemplated once that she was immune and would never fall for anyone.

Deep down, she feared that she wasn't normal.

†

The following day Lucy got up bright and early.

She peeked out of her window and gladness filled her soul as she could see the sun's rays peeking over the horizon, promising a glorious day. With each sunrise came the promise of a new beginning, a fresh start. The rising sun whispered secrets of hope, encouraging Lucy to embrace the day's unknown adventures. It was a gentle reminder that life was a tapestry of moments, each as beautiful and unique as the morning sun. After showering, she opted for her most comfortable pair of jeans and a pastel yellow tank top. The spaghetti straps of her top revealed long, slender arms.

She enjoyed a breakfast of bacon and eggs, alone, and then went to her mother's room. She was still sleeping, but very restless, and appeared to be in insurmountable pain. Her medication was on the bedside table, so Lucy removed it and went through all the directions. On a piece of paper, she created a timetable, so that she would be able to administer everything correctly. Angela moaned, so Lucy walked to her side. She took her mother's cold hand between her warmer ones.

"Good morning," she said.

"Are you still here? I thought you were leaving," Angela muttered. Her facemask oxygen had been replaced by nasal prongs, so it was easier to hear what she was saying.

"I can see you need taken care of. Like it or not, I'm your private nurse from now on. And no, you don't have to pay me. I want nothing from you. I'm just here out of obligation, as you are, after all is said and done, still my mother."

Her wrinkled eyes filled with liquid. Lucy ignored the tears and handed her the medication that was due, which she took with shaky fingers. Pressing the button on her bed made the headpiece lift her into a sitting position, and made it easier for Lucy to pop them into her mouth. She accepted the water Lucy offered her and swallowed the tablets down with some difficulty. The morphine syrup was four hourly, so Lucy made a mental note to get a morphine PCA pump installed instead. As the pain became worse, the medication would need to be increased. Soon her mother's two carers walked in and introduced themselves as Claire and Gwen.

Lucy greeted them and after a bit of small talk, she said, "I'm going to arrange IV morphine for her. It will be administered through a pump, and she'll have a button so she can administer small amounts of morphine by pressing the button whenever she's in pain. And don't worry, the pump has a safety feature, which will prevent her from overdosing. It only administers as much as the maximum dosage. I'll connect the IV line to her chemo port that's here in her chest."

"I've worked with those before," Claire said. "I'll teach Gwen so that she also knows how to change the bags and everything."

Claire was a young woman, in her early twenties with long black hair and green eyes. Gwen appeared slightly older with brown curly hair that had started greying at the roots.

"Can you two have her cleaned up while I call the doctor?"

"Of course," Gwen said.

While they washed Angela, Lucy called her doctor, who was there within the hour, and they had the PCA pump set up and running in no time. Dr. Brown was an impeccably dressed man. His suit was made from the finest fabrics, and fitted him like a glove, accentuating his physique. Lucy guessed he was about her mother's age.

After they were done with Angela, he led her out of the room and closed the door. He spoke in a gentle tone that carried a soothing melody. "I took your mom for a follow-up PET scan last week and I have some bad news. Sadly, her cancer has spread. It has metastasized to her lungs, which is why her chest is so wheezy and tight. We've commenced with ozone therapy, which is making the world of difference, but she doesn't have long left."

Lucy nodded her understanding. "How long do you think she has?"

"Not long. I'm afraid. Weeks, maybe days. We have tried all avenues available to us. We've stopped the chemo because it wasn't making any difference. She was on a trial for a bit, too. Unfortunately, all that's left now is palliative care. We have to try and keep her as pain-free and comfortable as possible. It's a good thing you're here." He gently patted her on the shoulder.

There were some legal issues when it came to IV morphine, so Lucy had some paperwork to complete.

After all the admin was done, she decided to take a walk around the gardens to get some fresh air. She walked the same path Robert had taken her on the day she had arrived and found one of the hidden nooks she so badly wanted to explore. The trees surrounding her were tall and dense, and right in the center was a bench. She sat for a long while, breathing the fresh air, revitalizing her senses. Lucy closed her eyes, savoring the sweet aroma of dew-kissed grass, which mingled with the scent of wildflowers that blossomed at her feet. She reveled in the calmness surrounding her, feeling as though time had temporarily suspended itself to allow her the opportunity of witnessing the beauty that nature brought. A cascade of warmth gently caressed her face as memories of her childhood filled her with melancholy. The sound of water splashing startled her, causing her to open her eyes. She got up and peered around the corner of the hedge and saw the shimmering of the pool water, the top moving in waves as if disturbed by an external force.

As she inched closer, she spotted Cameron lifting herself out of the water and moving lazily to the bar, laughing and talking to the beautiful young blonde Lucy had the displeasure of running into the previous day. Cameron sat beside her and sipped on a drink.

"Hey," she called out when she finally reached the duo.

Cameron's gaze shifted to her. "Hi. Didn't know you were up. This is Frankie."

"Hi, Frankie – or should I call you 'just leaving'? Thanks for popping by again, but Cameron and I have some things to discuss." Lucy turned to Cameron. "Frankie and I met yesterday, and she wasn't all that excited to meet me."

"Hi," Frankie responded with a shocked expression. "I guess you're the infamous daughter that everyone has been whispering about."

A wave of weariness washed over Lucy. "Cameron, I was under the impression that you and I had a deal. Didn't we agree to do this together? If you refuse to hold your end of the bargain, then I don't see the point of staying." Lucy bit her tongue, knowing she was completely out of line.

Frankie flashed a sarcastic grin. "Oh, come on. Relax. Grab a drink and join us. I suggest you go put on your bathing suit, because—as you can see—we have a lady in our midst." She motioned toward Cameron and added, "Swimming in the nude is not an option today."

"Lady?" Lucy placed her hands on her hips and rolled her eyes. She secretly wondered how well Frankie and Cameron knew each other. Not that it was any of her business. They seemed very comfortable around one another.

"I'm right here," Cameron mused with a sparkle in her eyes.

"I'll be right back. As the saying goes, if you can't beat them, join them." Lucy walked back toward the house.

She peeked through the doorway at her mother, who was sleeping soundly. The morphine must have done its magic. She then went up to her bedroom where she went straight to the window and looked down at the pool area. She had a perfect view of the entire garden and of the ocean in the distance.

The two of them were still looking very cozy by the bar. Lucy sighed. It was almost like she was sixteen again, and she didn't want to be there. Too much had happened, and she wasn't cut out for all the emotions she had been trying to suppress for so long. She threw herself onto her bed and lay on the cool linen for a few moments, contemplating her next step. She was behaving like a spoilt child, and she was embarrassing herself. The thought of the newcomer had her feeling extremely uncomfortable. Even though she didn't know anything about Frankie, there was something about her that Lucy just couldn't put her finger on. She swallowed hard, groaned as loud as she could and got up from her bed. Her bags had been unpacked by one of the staff, so she had to fumble through the dresser in order to find her bikini. Why was she allowing Cameron to boss her around? Why did it even matter that she had a friend over? She was free to be and do as she pleased, and Lucy had absolutely no right to behave like an immature brat.

After finding her swimwear, she donned her little two-piece, which probably didn't cover enough, and then walked back to the pool area. She noticed Cameron's eyes wandering over her exposed skin as she brushed past them and then bent over to retrieve a cold juice from the bar fridge. Before Frankie had any chance to oppose the idea, Lucy chose a bar stool right next to her and directed her attention to her. She had grey eyes, which were luminous in the sunlight.

"So, Frankie, what do you do for a living?"

She looked slightly uncomfortable but responded anyway. "I'm the rep who will be providing your mother's

IV morphine. I've been delivering all her medication since she became ill."

"Ah. I see. Which means that I'll be in contact with you when I need a refill. Good to know." She instantly felt stupid for her previous suspicions.

Cameron swiftly took a sip from her drink, got up, and dove into the pool.

Lucy watched as she swam and admired the way her perfect body sliced through the water. Her lean shoulders glistened when she resurfaced, and her back muscles moved when she wiped the water from her face.

When Frankie shuffled uncomfortably in the chair beside her, Lucy suddenly returned to reality, and noticed that she had been blatantly staring at Cameron, her lips slightly parted, and that she had stopped breathing. It took great effort, but she managed to turn her focus back on Frankie.

"How long have you known Cameron?" Lucy found it difficult to keep her voice level. After watching Cameron's half naked body, she was tormented by the images bouncing around in her head.

"We met here, at Angela's bedside a year ago."

"My mother has been sick for a *year* already?"

"Yeah, which I'm sure you would have known had you kept in touch, right?" The cruelty of her words cut right through Lucy.

"Not sure what they told you, but I did not leave voluntarily." Lucy played with her juice bottle, her fingers trembling.

Frankie lowered her voice momentarily. "Listen here, Lucy, your mother *hates* your guts. So does Cameron, so maybe you should just hop back on your broom and fly back to wherever the hell it is you hail from."

Her words struck an exposed nerve. "I'm not sure if you know this, Frankie, but Cameron is the one who invited me here. So, stay in your lane." Lucy narrowed her eyes when she spoke.

Frankie gasped. She remained dead quiet.

Lucy wasn't sure how long they sat there before a gentle voice brought her mind back to reality. "Can I get you another one?" Cameron was back from her swim.

Her eyes shot up at Cameron and she nodded. "Yes, please," Lucy said.

She placed another bottle of grape juice in front of Lucy. "There you go."

"Thanks," Lucy said, trying to ignore the lump that had formed in her throat, which was threatening to constrict her airway.

"Did you enjoy the swim, babe?" Frankie spoke to Cameron, the sweetness in her voice dripping like sticky honey.

Babe?

Cameron shook her head and answered, "It would've been much more fun if you'd joined me."

"I will next time, hun," Frankie said. She winked at Lucy, indicating her triumph.

"I'm going to tend to my mother. Later, guys." With that Lucy pushed herself away from the bar counter, stood from the barstool, and left them to it. On her way back to the house, she caught herself wondering if Cameron was watching her.

†

That night Lucy struggled to fall asleep, so the next morning when she got up, she was exhausted. After taking a cool shower, she headed down for breakfast. Up until then, she'd been having breakfast alone every time, but when she reached the dining room, Cameron was seated by the table. She looked strikingly beautiful wearing black slacks and a navy long-sleeve button-up shirt. The material clung to her curves, revealing every movement as she sipped on her coffee. A sleek watch adorned her wrist, adding a touch of luxury and sophistication. Confidence radiated from her poised demeanor. The sight of her made Lucy catch her breath. She was probably the most striking woman she had ever laid eyes on. Her hands looked manicured, but her nails were not varnished, and her gentle perfume reached Lucy's nostrils. She almost made Lucy feel plain in comparison.

Lucy realized that up until the day she had met Cameron she always had so much confidence, which was in serious jeopardy in Cameron's presence. She caught herself wondering whether she had made love with Frankie the previous day, and her stomach did a nauseous twist. She had no idea why that would bother her at all, but for some reason it really did. Cameron looked up at her when she sat in a chair across from her, and watched as Lucy poured some cereal into a bowl. Cameron was having fried eggs and toast, but Lucy wasn't in the mood for anything greasy.

"Good morning," Cameron greeted in a friendly tone. She had obviously slept better than Lucy had. A night of sex was always good to aide in insomnia. Lucy shrugged the thought away.

"Hi." She took a bite of the high-fiber cereal which tasted like hay and tried to return the smile, but she was sure that she failed.

"Good morning, sweeties."

Lucy cringed at the sound of Frankie's shrill voice and turned her head in the direction of the imposter who had just entered.

"Good morning, Frankie. Did you sleep well?" Cameron's voice still sounded cheerful.

"Oh, I slept like a goddess. Just knowing you're so close to me, babe."

"Don't you have a home?" Lucy shot at Frankie, instantly wishing she could keep her short temper at bay.

"Is rudeness a trait from where you're from? I am a pharmacist by trade, I could help, you know. With medication."

Cameron shifted in her chair, looking uncomfortable. She looked back and forth at them.

"I'm sorry. Unlike the two of you, I didn't sleep very well last night." Lucy sighed.

"Can we like at least try to be friends, Lucy?" Frankie's voice was as insincere as a smile on a Monday.

"Sure," Lucy said, even though she wasn't in the least bit interested. There was something about Frankie and it bothered her. Lucy generally liked all kinds of people and couldn't understand why she was feeling so opposed to Frankie's being there.

"Cool. Dude, I have some great vitamins that will help you cope during the day, if you want."

"Sure," Lucy said.

Cameron took a bite of toast, chewed twice and swallowed. "Great. Now that we all get along, we can focus on why we're here. Lucy and I can start with Angela's pressure care after breakfast. I'm ready when you are," Cameron directed at Lucy. She was obviously trying to cut through the heavy atmosphere the two women had created.

"All right," Lucy said before taking a few sips of her coffee. She then pushed her full bowl of cereal away.

"Not hungry? You didn't have dinner either. You should eat, you need your strength," Cameron said. Her voice sincere.

"Cameron is right. Dude, you do need to eat. Jus' sayin'." Frankie had poured herself some cereal and took a bite from her corn flakes.

"I have no appetite. I'll be hungry by lunch time, I'm sure." It wasn't like Lucy to not have an appetite, because she was, usually like all nurses were, always hungry.

"Maybe the vitamins will help your appetite, too," Frankie interjected after she swallowed.

"Sure." Lucy inhaled and gulped the rest of her coffee down.

They sat and waited for Frankie to finish eating. She crunched on her corn flakes like she was chomping on rocks. Her loud chewing tested Lucy's very last nerve.

Frankie slurped the last spoonful into her mouth when Cameron spoke.

"Ready?" She looked expectantly at Lucy.

"Yeah."

They got up and left Frankie at the table.

†

Angela looked pale. She wasn't eating well, and she was sleeping most of the time. All of this was aggravated by the morphine she pushed, which was causing her to fade bit by bit. She was pain free, though, so Lucy couldn't stop the morphine pump. While Cameron held her on her side, Lucy massaged some cream onto her back in order to help with the circulation. She glanced over at Cameron.

"Can we go for a walk after this?"

"I don't see why not."

It only took a few minutes to finish up with Angela, so they had two hours to kill before the next time she had to be turned again.

Claire and Gwen walked in. Lucy explained to them that Angela needed pressure care and how often it needed to be done. They agreed to assist with that when Lucy wasn't around.

"Shall we go?" Lucy asked Cameron, knowing that her mother would be in capable hands for a while.

"Absolutely."

Lucy led the way and Cameron followed her. They followed a cobblestone path that led to the fountain, which had a statue of a dolphin in the center. The water ran over the dolphin, and the fountain's surrounding wall was just high enough for them to sit on. The crystal-clear waters shimmered under the warm sunlight, reflecting the world above in a mesmerizing dance. The pond was home to a group of graceful and vibrant koi fish, whose presence enhanced the tranquility of the garden. Lucy sat down and splashed the water with her hand, watching as the ripples broke the picturesque reflection.

"So, what's the deal with you and Frankie?" she asked, while watching as the water's surface calmed again. She swirled her fingertips over the top of the water.

"We're just friends. Why?"

"Just want to know."

"She's actually not that bad once you get to know her."

"Are you lovers?"

Cameron shook her head and sat down next to her. She mirrored Lucy's movements and dipped her hand into the water. "She's not my type."

"Not pretty enough for you?" Lucy was only joking, but she answered anyway.

"She's pretty." Cameron shrugged. "I'm not shallow. I just prefer more mature women."

"Ah. So you *are* gay."

"Is that a problem for you?"

"I'm lesbian, too. I was just curious."

"Do you have a girlfriend back home?"

"Me?" Lucy laughed. "No, I'm single."

"Me too."

Lucy realized how childish she had been acting around Frankie and felt ashamed. She wasn't sure why it was so important to her that Cameron liked her, but it was. "How long have you been here?" She looked at her sideways as she asked the question that had been on her mind all week. Cameron seemed so at home there.

"Five years."

"That is a very long time. How did you end up working for my mother? All the way here from England?"

"I wasn't exactly prepared for an interview." She was deep in thought for a moment. "Well, let's see. How to make this long story short." She scratched her chin with her dry hand as she stared into the water. "I studied accountancy, hated the job, and then one day I saw an ad on the internet. Benefits and salary looked great. Took a shot at it and got the job immediately."

"It must have been a very lucrative package for you to leave your home country."

"It was. Excellent salary, a place to stay, free meals, servants. You know, these things look tempting when you're not used to that sort of lifestyle."

"Is that why you're still here? The comfort? Surely my mother doesn't need a personal assistant anymore?"

She frowned and turned to face Lucy. "So answer me this. Why were *you* never here? You never called, never wrote. Emails are quite easy to send, you know."

"I have my reasons." And she preferred them locked away.

"Come on, Lucy. All families have their differences. And not contacting your parents is inexcusable. Angela was… is like a mother to me. I guess since you were never present, I automatically took your place."

Lucy blinked. Her mother, who had so cruelly pushed her away, had accepted Cameron into her life, replacing her own daughter without a second thought. "You have—"

A noise stopped her from completing her sentence. She looked up and saw Frankie trudging around the corner, moving toward them. Frankie was in a short dress with very high heels, balancing on the cobblestone path. Lucy swallowed, shook her head and got up. She gave Cameron a hopeless look before she walked off toward the house.

Frankie frowned at Lucy as she walked past her, but Lucy wasn't in the mood for her false pretenses, so she ignored her, all the while fighting back the tears that were threatening to show.

†

Lucy stayed in her room for the remainder of the day, not once going down to help turn her mother. She hoped the carers would continue the basic care without supervision. The conversations of the day played over and over in her head, and left her feeling run down. Most people would say that she felt sorry for herself, but in fact, she was furious. Staying away was best, or else she would say things that she would later regret. It had started raining, with a hectic storm blowing in. She wished that she had someone to talk to. In the past, she would usually just go out, get drunk, and find a warm body for the night. Unfortunately, this was not an option. It was at seven pm that she heard a soft knock on her bedroom door. She got up and opened it by a crack. Cameron stood there, with a tub of chocolate ice cream and two spoons. Her eyes were filled with a quiet sadness that mirrored Lucy's distress. Even though Lucy wanted to grab her and hold onto her, while crying every unshed tear, she just managed to smile weakly.

Cameron raised the ice cream tub and rocked it from side to side. "This is a peace-offering."

"What for?" she asked before opening her door all the way and motioning for her to enter.

"You vanished without an explanation, so I wanted to check in. Thought you might be upset."

She strolled in and sat on Lucy's bed. Naturally, Lucy followed and sat beside her. Cameron was dressed in checkered pajama pants and a tank top. Her long legs stretched out in front of her. Lucy shifted up and leaned back against her pillows. She patted the spot next to her. "Sit here."

"Are you talking to me or the ice cream?"

"Both."

Cameron moved to position herself where Lucy had instructed her to sit. She offered one of the spoons.

The cold of the sweet dessert felt great on Lucy's tongue, and she suddenly realized how hungry she was. Except for the bite of "horse-food" she'd had that morning, she hadn't eaten anything all day. After she had retreated to her safe haven, she had taken a nap, completely missing mealtimes.

"Tell me what happened with you and your mother." Cameron leaned back into the pillows, casually eating a spoonful.

The warmth of her body was comforting. It took some restraint on Lucy's part to not lean against her and cuddle the way she used to with Paul. "Why?" she asked.

"You keep running away. Whenever I bring up the subject of you and your mother, you find a way to disappear. I have now cornered you and you can't escape this time. Besides, I have the ice cream." She wiggled the tub under Lucy's nose. "My weapon of choice."

"Ah. Bribery." Lucy dug her spoon into the tub and scooped a generous portion.

Cameron crossed her legs over by her ankles before leaning farther back into the pillows. She slurped at the frozen treat that had started melting and dripping from her spoon.

Lucy stared at her mouth for a second, her gaze following down over her breasts and then to her legs for a while, and then back up to her eyes. "Would you mind if we just enjoyed this beautiful treat that you so kindly brought up to my chambers?"

Cameron smirked. "It helps to talk about it."

"It wouldn't make any difference. I'm here and I'm doing what she wants. That's just going to have to be enough."

Cameron placed a reassuring hand on Lucy's arm. "That's okay. When you're ready to tell me, I promise I won't judge. I will just listen."

After eating most of the ice cream, Lucy placed her empty spoon down on her bedside table and leaned her head onto Cameron's shoulder. Lucy was sure she could hear her heart beating loudly and inhaled her scent slowly. "Thank you." She could feel Cameron tensing up, but instead of making any sudden moves, Cameron too placed her spoon down, together with the ice cream tub, and put her arm around Lucy's shoulders.

"You okay?" Cameron's voice was merely a whisper.

"This feels nice." Lucy leaned in completely and submitted to her embrace.

"I'm glad," she said.

They sat like that for a long time, no one saying a word, until Lucy found herself drifting off.

"I think it's best I leave," Cameron finally said.

"Wait." Lucy stopped her. "Would it be awkward if I asked you to stay for the night?"

"Why would it be awkward?"

"It's just that I haven't been sleeping well, and it feels so comforting with you here."

"Turn onto your side," Cameron instructed as she slid her arm in under the curve of Lucy's neck.

Lucy shuffled onto her right side and relaxed into her embrace, feeling Cameron's warm body behind her. While Cameron's right arm was under Lucy's neck, tucked underneath her pillow, her left arm wrapped around Lucy and pulled her tight into her. Even though it was difficult for Lucy to suppress the need growing from deep within her, she soon drifted off and slept better than she had in a long time.

†

The following morning, when Lucy woke up, Cameron was gone. She had taken the empty tub of ice cream, and their spoons were gone too. She stretched and looked at her phone. It was eight am. She had slept at least nine hours straight. Memories of Cameron's body snug against hers made her flush. In all her years of adulthood she had never once passed up on an opportunity to seduce someone for a night of meaningless sex, but there was something different about Cameron. After a quick shower, she opted for a short summer dress. The storm had cleared and the sunlight streaming in through the window promised a beautiful day. After applying a light layer of make-up, she went downstairs to get some breakfast.

When Cameron spotted her in the kitchen, her face lit up. She was standing at the stove, frying eggs. "How do you take your coffee?"

"Strong with extra milk, please."

She looked at her sideways. "You look beautiful."

Lucy blushed. "Thank you. Where's Connie?"

"It's Saturday. She has the day off. Can I make you some eggs?"

"Sounds great. Two sunny side up for me." Lucy popped some bread into the toaster and dug around the fridge for the butter. After placing the butter on the table, she took out two plates.

"I'll have mine scrambled." Frankie's unwelcome voice came in from the doorway.

Lucy sighed inaudibly and took out a third plate.

"Sure," Cameron said as she reached for the eggs.

"Dude, I have your vitamins." Frankie pulled a bottle of B-complex pills from the pockets of her tiny shorts and tossed it on the table. The plastic bottle landed with a thud and almost rolled off the other side, Lucy caught them just on time. "I hope those will help," Frankie said sweetly.

"Thanks." Lucy looked at the bottle for a second before placing it upright in front of her plate. "Are Claire and Gwen here today?" Lucy asked Cameron as she dished their eggs onto their respective plates.

"Yes, they are." Cameron whisked some eggs in a bowl and poured them into the pan before she added, "I have employed night staff to tend to your mom too. I just figured with the two-hourly turns and such."

"Good thinking. Thanks." Lucy placed a plate of toast on the table and proceeded to butter a slice.

Once Cameron was done with Frankie's scrambled eggs, the three of them sat down to eat.

Frankie scooped a large bite and shoved it into her mouth. "I was thinking," she said to Cameron with her mouth full, "how about you and I take the day and go do something?"

Lucy was sure she could detect some annoyance in Cameron's voice when she spoke.

"What did you have in mind?"

"I don't know, babe. Movie and lunch, maybe?"

Cameron hesitated for a moment and looked at Lucy.

Lucy continued eating and acting as though she wasn't fazed.

"I suppose we can," Cameron said.

Frankie squealed in delight. "Great, I can't wait."

Lucy finished her food in silence and after her last bite, she pushed her chair back and said, "Thank you for breakfast, Cameron." She placed her dishes in the dishwasher and left.

CHAPTER FOUR

It was Tuesday. A few days had passed since Frankie had asked Cameron out on a date. Lucy couldn't help but feel upset that she had gone. Since that beautiful night of sleeping in Cameron's arms, nothing much had happened. She had hoped that Cameron would show up at her door again, but to no avail.

On waking up, Lucy was determined to get her mother out of bed that day. Fresh air would be good for her, and Lucy realized that her mom might not have another chance to be outdoors.

She was the first at the breakfast table, and Connie made her eggs, bacon and toast. Just as she took her first bite, Cameron walked in, wearing a pair of jeans and a white tank.

Lucy's breath caught in her throat at the sight of her. Her hair was still damp, and she smelled of coconut shampoo. Cameron smiled when she sat down next to Lucy and pulled a bowl closer.

As Cameron reached for the high-fiber cereal, Lucy stopped her. "Don't have that cereal, it will turn you into a were-horse."

"That bad, huh?" Cameron pushed the box away and reached for a slice of toast on Lucy's plate. Lucy playfully slapped her hand away.

Just then Connie waltzed in carrying a plate for Cameron. "Thanks, Connie. You read my mind."

"I made extra, Cameron. I know how you like your breakfast," Connie said as she placed the plate down.

"You're my hero." Cameron spread butter on the toast and then looked up at Lucy. "You've been quiet lately."

"I've just been enjoying the gardens. I love nature. This place has changed so much over the years."

"It is breathtaking here."

"So how was your date with Frankie the other day?" Lucy asked as she watched her prep the perfect bite before placing it into her mouth.

She grinned. "It wasn't a date."

"Is she not joining us for breakfast?"

"She had to go to work a morning shift. She also helps out at the hospital pharmacy, but she'll be back later. Probably around lunchtime."

Lucy was relieved that they could spend some time together without Frankie constantly interrupting. "Great."

"So, are you ready for your mother?"

"I am. In fact, I was thinking. Today, we're trying a different approach," she said.

Cameron raised an eyebrow at Lucy's statement. "What are you planning?"

"I'm getting her out of bed."

"Sounds like a wonderful idea, but she's a very stubborn lady. Won't it be too strenuous for her?"

"I think the fresh air will be good for her. I'll get her into her wheelchair and take her outside for a bit. She'll probably resist at first, but I'm sure she'll end up enjoying it."

Cameron nodded thoughtfully. "I hope you're right. It's worth a try, especially if it will bring some joy to your mom. How can I help?"

Lucy smiled gratefully. "Thank you, Cameron. Having you there will make it easier. I'll place her wheelchair next to the bed, and you can help me get her ready. We'll take it slow and make sure she feels comfortable."

Cameron took her last bite of food and then got up. "Let's get to it then," she said with a mouth full of food, which she then swallowed without chewing.

"Chew your food, Cameron," Lucy said teasingly as she stood.

It was a warm and sunny day. Lucy's mother was in her usual position, curled up on her side.

Lucy touched her arm in order to wake her. "Come on, Angela, it's time to get you up." Angela opened her eyes and squinted at Lucy. "Don't be scared. We'll help you." Lucy supported her back and helped her into a sitting position. She didn't resist as Lucy had expected her to.

Cameron supported Angela while Lucy pulled the wheelchair closer to the bed. They then gently lifted Angela and placed her into the chair. Cameron was strong and Angela was skin and bone. The two of them lifted her like she was a small bag of feathers.

"Where are we going? Can't you just let me die in peace?"

"We're taking you outside. You can't lie here day after day. It's not good for you." Lucy spoke gently to her.

Cameron placed the foot pieces of the wheelchair down and put her feet on them. Her legs were light, but stiff. After they had secured her in, Lucy pushed her wheelchair outside. Angela's eyes narrowed as the sun reached her face.

Cameron placed a straw hat on Angela's head, and then a pair of sunglasses over her eyes. For a moment Lucy thought she recognized the mom she had once known. With the hat propped over her eyes and the familiar sunglasses, she was practically good as new. A familiar ache crawled its way into Lucy's heart, and she diverted her attention away, to stop the tears from coming. Her emotions were getting the better of her and she didn't like it one bit. She reminded herself that she hated her mother, and that she was just a patient. Nothing more, nothing less. Lucy pushed her chair all the way to the deck by the pool, and locked the wheels after she made sure she was in full shade. The last thing her mom needed now was sunburn. Cameron followed close behind and occupied a deckchair right next to Angela's wheelchair. She sat her perfect body down and took Angela's cold claw-like hand into her own.

Lucy took a seat on the deckchair next to Cameron and watched her talking to Angela softly, constantly reassuring her.

Angela stared at the pool and with a weak voice said, "Lucy?"

"I'm right here," Lucy said. Her voice gentle.

"Remember that dog we had… what was his name…"

"Bubbles?"

Angela laughed quietly. "That's right. Bubbles. Remember when you were little and trying to teach him to walk on a leash, but the sprinklers went on? Bubbles made a run for it, but instead of letting go of the leash, you held on for dear life and went sliding down the lawn after Bubbles. You had lost your balance and Bubbles pulled you all the way down to the edge of the lawn."

Lucy laughed. "Bouncing up and down over the hills."

"You were black and blue for days."

Lucy smiled. "It was totally worth it."

"After that event you begged me to sell the dog and buy you a cat."

Lost deep in thought, Lucy lowered her voice and said, "I miss Bubbles."

While raising her index finger and smiling playfully, Cameron piped in, "I had a fish called Bubbles." She went silent for a moment and then continued, "I wonder what happened to him…"

"He probably drowned," Angela said, struggling to laugh and coughed.

Cameron's lips curled up at the edges. "Naha, he was too good of a swimmer."

As they sat by the pool, Lucy watched as Cameron engaged Angela in conversation, sharing stories and memories that brought warmth to her mother's face. The pain in Lucy's heart began to subside, replaced by a bittersweet nostalgia. She listened intently as their laughter filled the air, her mother's weak voice recounting happy moments from their past.

Time seemed to slow down as they reminisced, their voices mingling with the gentle lapping of the pool water. Lucy felt a sense of connection and love she hadn't experienced in a long time. The weight of resentment lifted momentarily, replaced by a tenderness she had forgotten.

They continued to swap tales, sharing moments of laughter and occasional tears. Lucy could see the genuine care in Cameron's eyes as she held Angela's hand, offering comfort and reassurance. It was a sight that tugged at Lucy's heart, reminding her that compassion and love were still present, despite the pain.

Lucy got up and walked over to the pool and dipped her foot into the water. She heard Angela whisper to Cameron, "Push her in, I dare you."

"Don't you do it, Cameron!" Lucy called out, but she was too slow, as Cameron had already tackled her and pulled her with her body weight into the water. As Lucy came up for air, she climbed onto Cameron's shoulders and pushed her head under the water. With Lucy still seated on Cameron's shoulders, she laced her fingers around Lucy's knees and held her in place as she stood up, lifting her out of the pool. Her wet dress clung to her, leaving no room for imagination to her onlookers. She held onto Cameron's forehead and tightened her thighs around her neck.

"Are you trying to drown me, woman?" Cameron asked.

"Yeah, just like your fish." Lucy laughed and swung her body backward. With her hands still attached to Cameron's head and her thighs still clenching her neck, she went down with her. Cameron placed her hands onto Lucy's thighs and twisted her body around to swim up to Lucy's face. When Lucy felt Cameron's body pressed against hers, she opened her eyes under the water and saw Cameron looking at her.

With her arms wrapped around Cameron's shoulders, she lifted them out of the water. Their eyes locked for a brief moment, while the world disappeared around them.

"Are we swimming?" Frankie's voice cut like a blade.

Lucy dropped her hands and Cameron let her go. The moment was gone.

"*We're* not swimming. *They* are," Angela said.

Cameron smiled and splashed water onto Lucy's face before whispering into Lucy's ear, "Your mom is so wise."

Frankie pulled her dress over her head and dropped it to the ground. "Don't mind if I do." She tiptoed onto the step of the pool in nothing but her lacy underwear.

Cameron cleared her throat and turned to face away from Frankie.

Lucy noticed Cameron looking uneasy and her face turning crimson. It was obvious to Lucy that she was uncomfortable, and Lucy immediately felt the need to protect her from the awkwardness. She turned to Frankie and repeated the same words Frankie had said a few days before. "I suggest you go put on your bathing suit, because—as you can see—we have a lady in our midst."

Cameron looked at Lucy and smiled. "Shall we go and get lunch?"

Frankie's face dropped as she watched Cameron and Lucy climb out and push Angela's wheelchair back into the house.

After putting Angela back into her bed, Lucy and Cameron walked past the window facing the pool. They watched for a moment as Frankie continued pretending to swim.

"I'll go get her," Lucy said. "I thought she was going to join us for lunch."

†

They enjoyed a quiet lunch, after which Lucy decided to go for a walk. She needed to clear her head. The memories her mother had brought up earlier had stirred some unwanted feelings from her past. Clouds were moving in, which was welcome after the hot day in the sun. She followed the tiny cobblestone path that led all the way to the end of the estate where she could look down at the sea below. It was the most peaceful piece of heaven, and she could be there by herself for hours, to reflect. Undetected.

The dark blue ocean stretched all the way to the edge, as far as the eye could see, and she inhaled the fresh ocean breeze that blew up the cliff. Lucy sank down onto a flat rock, and just breathed for a moment. Waves crashed against the rocky shore below, filling the air with a symphony of sound and scent. Seagulls soared overhead, their calls blending harmoniously with the ever-present rhythm of the tide.

Lucy had always been drawn to the ocean. It held an inexplicable power, enchanting and unpredictable, at once captivating and humbling. She often found solace in its presence, a respite from the chaotic whirlwind of life. Today, she sought solace yet again, eager to find a moment of clarity amidst the ebb and flow.

As she gazed into the vast blue expanse, she imagined the secrets the ocean held within. The cool, fresh air washed away all her anger and regrets.

A droplet landed on the tip of her nose. With a deep breath, Lucy closed her eyes, grounded once again in the present moment. Without thinking, nor feeling anything but freedom, she sat there and enjoyed the trickle of rain on her face. Nothing could harm her there, and all she wanted to do was just stay there and never leave. She felt home, which was absurd seeing as this wasn't her home anymore. Jumping off a cliff had never been more tempting, and for a short moment, she truly felt like she had nothing to lose and wondered if anyone would even miss her, besides Paul. One of those tears that she had been trying to suppress slipped over her cheek, down her face, leaving a hot trail and she basked in the coolness the wind brought over the wetness it left on her skin. She had never been the depressed type before, and this sudden eruption of self-pity caught her by surprise.

The faint sound of footsteps falling on soft grass behind her quickly brought her mind back to reality. She looked around with burning eyes and saw Cameron approaching. With quick movements, she dried her eyes and faced the ocean again, hoping the rain would cover the evidence of her sadness. She didn't want Cameron to see her at such a vulnerable state, because she didn't want her to think that she was weak. The rock Lucy sat on was big enough for them both, but it would be a tight squeeze.

Without hesitation, Cameron walked up to her resting place, and sat down beside her. She faced the sea. "It's beautiful out here, isn't it?" She spoke softly.

Lucy could hear her exhale slowly beside her and it made her shiver with want. Cameron's knee grazed against hers, sending an electric current through her. "Absolutely magnificent," she said before looking at Cameron. Her eyes followed the silhouette of Cameron's side profile, and she wanted to tell her the effect her presence had on her, especially sitting so close to her.

"Are you okay?" Cameron was still looking out over the ocean.

"Let's forget about me for a moment," Lucy said. "You were looking very uncomfortable around Frankie this afternoon. Did something happen?"

"Uh…" Cameron lowered her gaze. "She's been a bit more pushy than usual with me."

Lucy stiffened. "Is she trying to seduce you or something?"

Cameron shook her head. "I don't know what's going on with her. She's been hitting on me since we met, and I have always been completely honest with her, but it's almost like she just gets more desperate every time I decline her advances."

Lucy frowned. "That's not acceptable. I'm going to tell her to spend less time here."

"Your mom needs her. Besides, I can protect myself. I'm a grown woman."

"I know you are, but if she's overstepping boundaries, she needs to be put in her place."

"Don't worry about me, please, Lucy." Cameron sighed. "Are *you* okay?"

"Why wouldn't I be?" Lucy was still facing her, and Cameron turned to glance at Lucy sideways, placing a gentle hand on her knee. Lucy tried to control her breathing. Cameron's soft touch was more than she could handle.

"Lucy, I can see you've been crying. Your mother is dying. You know it's okay to be sad. Even though the two of you haven't gotten along for many years, she's still your family. She's your only family." She spoke gently. Her hand was still on Lucy's knee, her thumb swirling in circles, caressing her softly.

Lucy stood and paced the edge of the cliff. "She's not my family. Family doesn't do what she has done to me."

"Lucy…" Cameron got up and closed the distance between them.

"She's…" Lucy sighed.

Cameron tried to take her hands. "Talk to me," she pleaded.

"I came here to be alone. Don't follow me." She pulled her hands back and stormed back toward the house.

Once in her room, as Lucy was closing the door behind her, Cameron gently pushed the door open and stepped into the room with her. She closed the door behind her quietly and walked up to Lucy's bed. She sat down and said, "I'm not leaving. I won't say anything, but I'm not leaving you alone like this."

Lucy dropped down beside her. She fumbled with her hands and didn't know what to say, torn between the excitement of Cameron so close to her and the fear of allowing someone into her world. This was all new to her. She had no idea how to open up to people and just wanted the past to be forgotten. None of this was supposed to be her life. On the one side she wanted everything to just go back to normal, but on the other hand she had no idea how she could continue her life as it used to be. Everything inside her was changing. They sat quietly for a long time before Lucy finally spoke.

"If I hadn't gone to fetch Frankie for lunch, do you think she would still be swimming?"

Cameron snickered. "Glad to have you back." She wrapped an arm around Lucy's shoulders and pulled her close.

"I wish I could stop being so mean to her," Lucy said shaking her head.

Cameron placed a soft kiss on her temple and said, "We all have our reasons."

CHAPTER FIVE

The following morning, Lucy awoke to the sound of a door closing softly. That was strange, as the cleaning staff never entered her room while she was asleep. She frowned and sat upright in her bed. That was when she spotted the envelope on her dressing table. She got up, picked it up and examined it. No name, no return address, nothing, so she opened it and pulled the paper out from within. She unfolded the page. It was an A4 paper with letters printed in bold:

Go home! Or suffer the consequences!

She ran to check the hallway, but there was no sight of anyone. Wow, someone wanted her out. Cameron? Frankie? After staring at the warning in her hands for some time, she refolded it and placed it back inside the envelope. Still frowning, she walked over to her window and looked down below. She saw Cameron with Frankie, talking animatedly by the koi pond. She needed to hear what the conversation was about, so she sneaked downstairs and into the garden. She followed the path that led to the pond and crept quietly until she could make out their voices.

"Ever since she came, you've, like, changed. I feel like we're drifting apart. Babe, go out with me tonight, forget her, she's trash. God knows what diseases you can get from her." Frankie sounded upset.

"Don't speak about her like that." Cameron's voice was firm. "You don't even know her."

"Well, neither do you, babe. I'm telling you, I'm getting a really bad vibe. Since she came you don't spend any time with me anymore. You don't swim with me anymore. You're always with *her*. I miss us."

"We're not having this conversation."

Lucy heard someone get up and walk away. She rushed back up to her room, not wanting anyone to see that she had been snooping.

†

After a long, cool shower, Lucy dressed in black trousers and a green button-up blouse. Her wet, shoulder-length blond hair hung like silk, dripping water down her back. As she looked at herself in the mirror, she couldn't help but wonder what Cameron would think. She was slightly shorter than Frankie, but not by much. She knew she wasn't bad looking, but she felt pale in comparison to Frankie, who appeared to be about ten years younger than she was. Even though she hadn't been jogging much lately, she also hadn't been eating well, so she had definitely lost some weight. Paul would have had a hissy fit if he knew that she wasn't looking after her health, so she decided against mentioning it to him. The note was tucked away safely in her dresser drawer, but not forgotten. After she was pleased with her outfit, she went down to the den, and upon passing her mother's room, she heard whispering coming from within. She froze and leaned with her ear closer to the partially open door. Was that Frankie's voice?

"I'm not convinced this is a good idea..." Cameron spoke quietly. "She's not how you said she is... She'll never do it."

"No, I think she is like *so* capable," Frankie said. "Dude, this nice person routine is, like, just a front."

"She hates me enough." Was that her mother?

"No, she doesn't hate you," Cameron spoke softly.

"Shhh..." Someone whispered, and then Lucy heard footsteps moving closer from the inside, so she made a run for the parlor. By the time the door swung open, Lucy was nowhere in sight.

Something was amiss, and the feeling grew stronger with each passing second. They were definitely up to something. This all felt like an ambush. Lucy's pulse raced and she wiped at the perspiration that had just covered her brow.

"There you are." Lucy jumped in surprise when Cameron shot her head around the corner. "How are you feeling?"

"Were you in my room this morning?"

"Not since last night. Why?" Her eyebrows crinkled together.

"Thought I heard something." Lucy walked over to the couch and sat down.

Cameron followed and sank down beside her. "Now it's your turn to answer my question. How are you feeling?"

"Hmm… Hungry."

"Want to go see what Connie has on the menu for today?"

"Actually, how about we go out to eat? Just you and I?"

"Are you asking me out on a date?" Her eyes lit up. "Mmm what are your intentions? Do you want to marry me? Make an honest woman out of me?"

"No. I prefer my women dishonest." She shoved Cameron with her shoulder.

"Dishonest, hey? Fine, in that case I don't find you attractive at all."

Lucy blushed but remembered the hushed conversation in her mother's room and reminded herself not to get too attached.

†

When Lucy climbed into her mother's Jeep Rubicon, she placed her feet on the dashboard, connected her Bluetooth to the car and blasted her favorite playlist over the speakers. She noticed Cameron glancing at her sideways and a smile played at the corners of her lips. Lucy sang along loudly and found joy in Cameron's amusement.

When they reached the waffle house, Cameron leaned over and looked at the screen of Lucy's phone. "You should send me your playlist." She clambered out of the car and led the way to the entrance of the restaurant.

Lucy felt proud that someone else in the world enjoyed the same music she did.

"Good morning. Table for two?" The waiter at the door looked to be in his mid-twenties.

"Yes, please," Lucy said. "A window seat will be great."

"Follow me," he said as he took two leather-bound menus and led the way.

Their table was private, and they had a breathtaking view of the ocean.

"My name is Stephen and I'll be your waiter today."

"Stephen, two strong coffees, please. Extra milk for the lady," Cameron ordered.

Stephen nodded politely and left.

Cameron looked striking in a pair of tight-fitting jeans, and a soft white shirt which complimented her tan. Her smile looked genuine when she looked at Lucy from across the table. "So, what do you want to eat?"

"This place makes the best crispy honey bacon. I will have that," she said without looking at the menu. "I always ate that here as a child."

Stephen returned with their coffees. "Ready to order?" he asked.

"I'll have the Hunny Oinky Waffle," Lucy said.

Stephen scribbled her order onto his notepad and looked at Cameron.

"I'll have what she's having," Cameron said before passing the menu to the waiter.

The restaurant owner stopped by their table and introduced himself to Cameron. When his eyes locked on Lucy, he froze. "Wow, you look incredibly familiar."

"George, it's me, Lucy. Remember? I used to come here all the time when I was little."

"Are you Mr. and Mrs. Donald's kid?" The shock in George's face was evident.

Lucy nodded politely. "In the flesh."

He gasped. "But didn't you drown? They told me you were dead."

Cameron choked on her coffee and squinted at Lucy.

Lucy responded, "Hmm. I'm still here. Alive and well."

"I'm glad to see that. Albeit confused. But good to see you again." He walked away awkwardly.

"Please don't tell me I'm sitting here having breakfast with a ghost," Cameron said with curiosity.

"Have you taken your loony meds today?" Lucy tapped Cameron on her arm and smiled.

"I'm guessing you're going to tell me to not ask you any questions."

"You know it."

There was a long moment of silence.

"This is a lovely place. I've been here before, once or twice. But generally, I don't get out much." Cameron played with the cutlery that had been placed in front of her.

"That tends to happen when you're living in a mansion where all your needs get tended to."

"It's not that. I guess since your mom became ill, I have been spending a lot of time arranging things for her. It hasn't been easy and there hasn't been time to socialize."

"I'm sorry, I didn't realize…" Lucy's voice drifted off. A tinge of guilt crept its way into her belly, but she shrugged it off instantly.

"Hey, it's part of the job I signed up for." Cameron's fingers danced from the cutlery she had been playing with to her napkin.

Lucy's eyes shot up just as Stephen approached holding their food.

"Wow, that was quick," Lucy said as he placed the plate in front of her. "Thank you, Stephen."

As they ate, Lucy gazed out the window at the resplendent ocean view while her mind drifted to the note, and all the hushed conversations that morning. The quiet discussion in the room earlier had been playing over and over in her head, and she just couldn't get to the bottom of it. She had no idea how to broach the subject to get a straight and honest answer out of Cameron. Were they hoping that she would sign away her inheritance, because her mother didn't have the mental capacity to do so? Lucy really didn't want any money from her family, but she also didn't like being taken advantage of.

She leaned forward, and looked at Cameron who was obviously enjoying her breakfast. "Enjoying that?"

"You were right, this is absolutely out of this world."

"I'm always right," Lucy had a sparkle in her eyes when she spoke. "Tell me about your family."

"Another interview? How come you get to ask all the questions, yet don't want to tell me anything?"

"You know who my mother is. Now tell me about yours."

"My mother died when I was eleven," she said without hesitation.

"Oh my god. I am so sorry." Lucy reached out and touched her hand.

Cameron looked at her and smiled sadly. "I don't remember much about her, because before she passed, she wasn't around much."

"What happened to her, if I may ask?"

Cameron swallowed loudly and pulled her hand away. "A drug overdose."

"Oh no, that's terrible, Cameron," Lucy breathed. "I'm so sorry..."

"My mom was a recovered drug addict when she met my dad, but after I was born, she developed post-partum depression. She would disappear for months at a time. My dad spent most of his married life searching for her. I believe she was shooting heroin. My dad took her to rehab clinics, tried to get her to clean up, but she kept absconding. She would show up at times, but only to steal. My dad caught her in the act once. She was selling her body for drugs. He never gave up on her. Took her straight back to rehab every time, only for her to relapse again—"

"Here you go, guys. A complimentary dessert from the owner."

"Thanks," Cameron said as a bowl of strawberries and cream was placed in front of her.

"George mentioned that this was always your favorite treat as a kid," Stephen said as he placed one in front of Lucy.

"It most certainly was." Lucy smiled her thanks and waited for Stephen to leave before speaking. "That must have been really horrible, Cameron. I'm so sorry that happened to you. Do you still speak to your dad?"

"I do. I visit him once a year."

Lucy played with her strawberries for a while. She decided to lighten the mood. "Ask him about Bubbles when you see him again—"

"What the ..." Frankie's voice spilled over Lucy's last words.

Frankie had once again appeared out of nowhere. Lucy noticed a man at her side. He looked to be in his early thirties, with brown hair, neatly cut, and matching brown eyes. Besides the stylish goatee, his face was smooth and clean.

"Dudes, meet my date, Dick," she introduced him.

Lucy could see Cameron swallowing before talking. "Hi, Dick. Pleased to meet you," Cameron said, and then directed her attention to Frankie. "Hi, Frankie. What are you guys doing here?"

"Dick asked me out and, dude, you know how much I, like, totally love the food here," she purred. "Can we join you guys?" She then looked at Dick, snapped her fingers and said, "Dick, chairs. Pronto."

Dick looked slightly uncomfortable, but he quickly grabbed two chairs from the closest unoccupied table and offered her one.

Frankie placed her chair right next to Cameron's, who shifted uncomfortably.

Stephen brought two menus for them and explained the specials to them.

"I'll have what Cameron had," Frankie said.

"I'll just have a waffle with vanilla ice cream, thank you," Dick said.

"Of course," Stephen said before he retrieved their menus and disappeared to the kitchen.

"So, what did I miss?" Frankie enquired.

Cameron gave Lucy a desperate look but didn't respond.

"Oh. Okay, don't tell me then," she said to Cameron and then looked at Lucy. "Your mother was calling for you when you decided to run off this morning. You were invited for a reason, not for a vacation." She turned back to Cameron. "Ooh. Strawberries and cream. Gimme, gimme." She pouted her lips at Cameron, as if waiting for her to place one into her mouth.

"You may have all of it," Cameron said as she slid her bowl toward Frankie.

"So, what do you do for a living, Dick?" Lucy looked at the guy who had long been forgotten by his date.

"I'm an architect," he answered and smiled at Lucy.

"Wow, how interesting. Have you designed anything we know?"

"In fact, I helped with the renovations on your mother's house," Dick said.

"Aw, and you did a great job, babe." Frankie spoke in a condescending manner to him while patting him on the shoulder.

"Is this your first date?" Lucy asked, focusing her attention on Dick.

"We've known each other for years. Frankie is my best friend's sister. We go way back when." Dick smiled at Frankie briefly.

"Your name, Dick, is it short for something?" Lucy asked.

"Believe me, he is like *so* not short for anything." Frankie giggled.

Dick shifted in his chair. He looked embarrassed. "My real name is Richard, but everyone calls me Dick."

Lucy emptied the last of her coffee and glanced at Cameron, relieved she was also done with hers. She was more than ready to get out of there. After Cameron reached for her wallet and took out the correct amount of money for their meals, including a decent tip, she placed it on the table. "It was really nice meeting you, Dick," she said as she got up and reached for Lucy's hand. "Shall we?"

"We shall," she said as she pushed her chair back and stood. "Enjoy your breakfast," Lucy said to them and followed Cameron out the door.

While still gently holding onto her hand, Cameron asked, "Did you have a good time?"

"I did, but the day is still young. Want to take a walk on the beach?" She looked hopeful as she asked the question.

"Would absolutely love to." Cameron let go of her hand, removed her shoes, unlocked the car, opened the trunk and tossed her shoes inside. Lucy followed suit.

They followed the short path from the car to the beach and once they reached the shore, they walked while the water licked at their feet.

The weather was mild, and there was only a slight breeze pushing in from the ocean. Lucy paused for a moment and looked out over the water. As the sun peeked timidly above the horizon, the world ignited with golden hues, and a cascade of warmth gently caressed her face. The vibrant colors rippled across the water. After about a minute, she continued to stroll, enjoying the fresh salty air, when they came upon a dead, washed up shark.

"Wow, it's a Ragged Tooth Shark, check it out." Cameron knelt beside it, inspecting it closely.

"Yeah, these are the critters that make me hesitant to swim in the sea," Lucy mumbled, still standing a step away.

"Contrary to popular belief, the Ragged Tooth Shark doesn't eat or even bite humans. They prefer seafood. Tiny little fish. Sushi."

Lucy laughed and admired her as she was still kneeling next to the fish.

"Unfortunately, this one has already crossed over." Cameron stood. "Hey, we should take it home, and cook soup with it," she teased.

"And then invite someone over to dinner that we don't particularly like?" Lucy snorted at her.

Cameron laughed and stepped closer to her. She pulled her closer by her blouse. Their faces were only inches apart, and Lucy had to focus really hard not to crush into her and devour her lips. "You can feed it to your mother," she whispered.

Lucy pulled away and playfully slapped her on the chest. "Race you to the car?"

†

"Hot chocolate?" Lucy offered as they walked into the kitchen.

"Mm. Yes, please." Cameron followed her to the kettle and watched Lucy switch it on. "I'll get the cups," she said as she reached up and removed two mugs from the shelf. Her body moved gracefully as she placed them down in front of Lucy. Her arm brushed against Lucy making her body want more.

Lucy scooped the powder into the cups before she said, "Thanks for a great morning. I really enjoyed it."

"I had a wonderful time, too. Pity about Frankie showing up. I had no idea she would gate crash our date."

"It wasn't a date." Lucy looked sideways at Cameron and winked playfully.

The kettle whistled as the water started to boil, so Lucy picked it up and poured the steaming liquid into the mugs while stirring the chocolate mixture, enjoying the aroma that came with it.

She handed Cameron her drink, which she took with eagerness. "I don't understand," she said. "It's called hot chocolate, but it's a liquid."

"As opposed to?" Lucy looked confused.

"Chocolate that has been warmed up." She grinned.

"That'll just make you sick. Shut up and drink what I gave you," Lucy said and laughed.

"It's delicious, thank you."

"Going to check on my mother. Care to join?"

Cameron nodded and followed her to Angela's room, where her mother was having lunch.

"Everything good?" Lucy asked Claire.

"Yes, your mom is eating well."

"That's great to hear," Lucy replied, relieved. "She seems to be in good spirits today."

Cameron observed Angela, who sat in her recliner with a smile on her face while slowly savoring each bite. "Your mom looks so content," Cameron remarked softly.

Lucy nodded, her eyes filled with a mixture of emotions. "I'm glad she's doing well. It hasn't been easy, but it's moments like this that make it all worth it."

†

That night, as Lucy entered her bedroom, she stepped onto a piece of paper in the doorway. She bent down to pick it up, immediately knowing it was another threatening letter. She unfolded the A4 printout.

I warned you, now it's time for our final game.

Her heart hammered in her chest. Sweat trickled her brow. She peeked out of her doorway and looked down the passage, but there was no one. Trembling, Lucy clutched the letter, desperate for any clue that could help solve the mystery of who was tormenting her. The words on the paper seared into her mind, resonating with a chilling certainty that danger was lurking in the shadows.

Fear consumed her, but there was also a flicker of defiance. She refused to uproot her life for an unknown threat. She read the letter again, before adding it to the drawer where the other note was.

After a quick shower, she lay alone in bed. Despite the angst in her chest, her mind kept wandering to Cameron. She pictured her attractive physique, the captivating look in her eyes whenever they locked gazes. At one point, she drifted off, only to awaken a few minutes later. The digits on her bedside clock seemed motionless, as she struggled to find solace and sleep. She was drenched in sweat, tormented by a pounding headache, and her stomach had begun to ache.

Glancing at the clock, she noted it was already four am, leaving her feeling frustrated. The stomach cramps intensified into nauseating waves, with recurrent bouts of vomiting, until she finally managed to find some respite and fall asleep.

The following morning, she woke up feeling thoroughly exhausted and dehydrated. After showering and getting dressed, she made her way down to the kitchen. A cup of soothing chamomile tea might help alleviate her discomfort. Her legs quivered, and her stomach continued to throb as if agonizingly stabbed. After pouring herself a cup, Lucy proceeded to her mother's bedroom. She settled into the chair beside her bed and sipped her tea slowly, seeking solace. Her mother appeared serene, and despite the lines on her face, her beauty still radiated. Memories flooded Lucy's mind of her mother once being the most stunning woman in her world. The heartbreak she experienced when her mother had sided with her father's decision to send her away seemed unbearable. Lucy gently held her mother's frail hand, squeezing it tightly. A tear fell onto her lap, mingling with the pain she held inside. How could her mother have been so cruel?

Angela stirred, causing Lucy's heart to skip a beat. "Cameron?" Angela whispered weakly.

"No, it's only me. Lucy," she responded softly.

Angela's fingers curled around Lucy's hand, and as she breathed steadily, her eyes closed once again. That's when the floodgates opened, and Lucy's body shook uncontrollably with her sobs. She wept for the years of separation, for the moments missed with her mother, and for the aspects of her mother's life that would forever remain unknown. Despite the resentment that simmered within her, Lucy cried because, deep down, she still loved her mother. After all, she was her mom. Lucy yearned to be in her presence, to share laughter and spend time together. Lucy wept until her eyes were swollen and burning, with a newfound disregard for who might witness her in such a state.

"You'll get snot all over yourself if you don't stop crying," her mother murmured. Only then did Lucy realize that her mother was awake. She sniffed and stood up, making her way to the bathroom. The cold water splashed onto her face offered a respite, and she blew her nose hastily.

Upon leaving the bathroom, Lucy noticed that Cameron had joined Angela's side. She was speaking to her in a gentle tone, assisting her with sips of water through a straw. A twinge of envy flickered inside Lucy as she observed their close relationship.

"Oh. Good morning." Cameron looked up at her. She looked fresh and ready for the day. "Did you sleep well?"

"Nope," Lucy murmured.

"You look like crap," Cameron teased, but she sounded worried.

"Don't speak to me like that," Lucy's mother muttered.

Cameron laughed. "I wasn't speaking to you, Angela. I was referring to your daughter over there."

"Thanks for the compliment, Cameron," Lucy mumbled and went to stand next to her mother's bed, on the opposite side of where Cameron stood.

"You're still beautiful, though," Cameron remarked at Lucy.

"Shut up," Lucy grumbled, assuming she was being sarcastic. "Do you want to watch the sunrise today, Mom?" Lucy asked, but without waiting for an answer, she started to prepare her wheelchair.

"No, please just leave me be. Let me die, please. I don't deserve to live." Her voice cracked and Lucy noticed that her cheeks were getting wet. She was crying.

"Don't say those things. I'll hear none of it. You're getting up." Lucy ignored her mother's pleas as she helped her out of bed and placed her gently into the wheelchair. After strapping her torso in and putting her feet up, Lucy pushed her out of her depressing bedroom. Cameron went ahead and unlocked the patio doors so that they could get outside. Lucy pushed the wheelchair out over the lawn, all the way to where she and Cameron had sat at the edge of the estate previously. The grass was still wet, and the sun had barely started peeking over the edge of the horizon. Lucy secured her wheels, and then took a seat on the rock. Cameron went to sit beside her without saying a word, and once again her closeness made Lucy's heart skip a few beats.

The heat radiated off Cameron's skin, in turn penetrating Lucy's soul. Cameron was dressed in black slacks and a black tight-fitting shirt. She smelled of coconut and toothpaste. The brilliant colors dancing over the ocean were magnificent, and the air was cool and fresh. They listened to the birds beginning to move and chirp as the world started awakening. But the sound most beautiful to Lucy was the sound of Cameron breathing beside her. Their shoulders brushed against each other, and every move she made was enticing. Lucy closed her eyes and breathed in her presence. She wanted Cameron around her, with her, beneath her. When Lucy opened her eyes again, she caught her mother looking at them. Her mother smiled for a short moment and then returned her gaze to the ocean.

"How's the new medicine working for you, Angela?" Cameron broke the silence after a long while.

Angela's head bobbed up and down. "The pain is more bearable. Much easier to deal with."

"That's good to hear. It was all Lucy's idea, right Lucy?" Cameron's eyes danced over Lucy's face.

"I don't like it when my patients are in pain." Lucy enjoyed the praise for a moment, especially coming from Cameron.

"You're a good nurse, Lucy." Cameron's voice was sincere.

"I know." Lucy smiled at her.

"It takes a very special person to do what you do."
Cameron touched her arm as she spoke.

"It's not an easy job, but someone's got to do it."

"You can nurse me back to health anytime," Cameron
said with a naughty look.

"And I just might."

"I'm very proud of the woman you've become,"
Angela spoke. Her voice gentle and filled with emotion.

Lucy almost fell off the rock when her mother uttered
the words. How she had longed to hear those words fifteen
years ago when she was all alone in the great big world. That
time when she had no one to run to. All she had was a little
granny flat in a stranger's yard. The old lady who had so
kindly offered her a safe place to stay when she had been
abandoned by her only family. The pain inside of Lucy
poured over the rim and flowed out in anger.

"Do you remember that night I called? Two months
after you and my father kicked me out?"

Angela's eyes widened. "You called?"

"Father answered the phone and told me never to call
again..."

"He never told me." Angela choked back tears.

"You ignored me when I was begging you for help. I
was left to deal with the mess all on my own. I almost bled to
death when I lost the baby."

"You lost the baby?" Tears streamed down Angela's
face.

Lucy could feel Cameron tense beside her but continued. "Thank goodness I did. What would I have done if I hadn't lost it? I was sixteen, pregnant with a baby that I didn't want."

"Lucy, your father didn't mention that you called."

"Even so, you never checked on me. Since I've been here, you never once asked if you had a grandchild."

Her mother was crying profusely. "Lucy, I'm so sorry. I wish I could turn back the clock." Her sobs racked her torso.

Cameron sat quietly without uttering a word. Her silence spoke louder of her understanding than her words could.

"You can't, Mom. What's done is done." Lucy blinked back a stray tear.

"Please forgive me," Angela choked on her sobs.

"How? How do I forgive?"

Her mother cried for a long time.

Lucy watched as the tears wet her gown and felt horrible that the confrontation had happened in front of Cameron. The words she had been holding back for years were out. There was nothing she could do to take them back.

After sitting in silence for a long while, Cameron leaned in and gave her a kiss on the side of her head. "Are you okay?" she whispered so Angela wouldn't hear. Lucy didn't respond. She just shook her head. "Are you hungry yet?"

"Famished," Lucy said. "Shall we go get breakfast?" Lucy stood and cleared her throat before walking over to her mother and unlocking her wheelchair. "It's getting hot; we should move to the shade."

"Of course," Cameron agreed and got up. She took the wheelchair from Lucy and moved Angela to the pool area. After ensuring she was well in the shade, she locked the wheels again. Lucy followed right behind them.

Connie walked up to them moments later. "Can I bring your breakfast outside today? I made muffins."

"Sounds lovely," Cameron spoke first. "I'm starved and I'm sure you guys are too." She directed the question at Lucy and Angela.

Angela mumbled, "I haven't had a muffin since... I can't remember."

Connie disappeared and returned a while later with a trolley, stocked with blueberry muffins, freshly squeezed orange juice, flasks with coffee, tea, and fresh fruit salad. Lucy took a muffin, which still felt warm from the oven, and handed it to her mother.

"Thanks," Angela said and took the muffin with trembling fingers.

Lucy watched as she tried to take a bite, but when she failed to keep her hand steady enough, she helped her by feeding her. Cameron's eyes never left them for a second as Lucy sat there, feeding her mother. When she was done, Lucy took a tray of food for herself and chose a seat next to

Cameron who was sitting in one of the lounge chairs with her breakfast.

"Mmm. This is delicious," Cameron said after she bit off a large piece.

Lucy took a big bite and looked up when she heard a familiar voice.

"Ooh, this looks divine, dudes."

"Morning, Frankie. Grab yourself a plate and come join us," Cameron said as she popped the last bite into her mouth and dusted off her hands.

"Cool, how can I say no to an invitation from you, babe?" She filled a plate with muffins and went to sit on the same sun lounger as Cameron.

Cameron shifted in order to make space for her.

"Frankie, if you need a place to sit, I'm done, you can have my place." Lucy stood and motioned to the now unoccupied space.

"No, I'm perfectly fine." She glanced at Cameron and winked.

Lucy sank back down hesitantly and asked, "How did the rest of your date go yesterday?"

"I think Dick's in love with me, but then again, who can blame him?" She pointed to her body. "I'm perfect, right?"

"What did you two love birds do?" Lucy ignored her vanity.

Cameron appeared amused at their exchange while sipping on her coffee.

"After a lovely breakfast, your choice was awesome, by the way, babe, we went to watch a movie at Dick's house. He couldn't keep his hands off me."

"A little too much information, Frankie." Lucy faked a shiver, smiled, got up, and went to pour herself a mug of coffee. When she was done, she returned to her spot. "Are you guys in love?"

"Love? No way. He's just a free meal."

"Kinda like this one?" Lucy asked before she could stop herself.

Frankie had just taken a gigantic bite and gasped as she lowered the food, almost choking.

"I'm so sorry, Frankie, it was a lousy joke. There's plenty for everyone to go around and more. I have no idea what possessed me to say that."

Frankie flicked her hair using her free hand. "Rude today, single tomorrow. Did your date yesterday not deliver?"

Cameron stood, placed her plate and mug back on the trolley and walked over to Angela. "Are you done, Angela? I think you could use some rest. Shall we go back inside?"

Angela shook her head. "And miss this? Not a chance."

Lucy drained her cup, got up and put her dishes on the trolley. "If you'll excuse me, Frankie. I'm going to help Cameron put my mother back to bed.

†

They put Angela back into bed and tucked her fleece blanket around her. After replacing her oxygen, Lucy reattached her IV line and connected her to the cardiac monitor. Angela fell asleep almost instantly.

Cameron touched Lucy's arm softly as they stood for a moment and watched her sleep. "You okay?" she asked softly. "That took great courage out there."

"Yeah, I'm just a bit tired today." Lucy spoke quietly so as not to wake her mother. "Come, let's go get some juice in the kitchen."

"You know the trolley's outside by the pool," Cameron said with a teasing tone.

"Do you mind if we don't right now?"

Her gaze softened. "What's up with you two? You've been at each other's jugulars since you met."

"I really wish I knew," Lucy said and turned to the door. Cameron followed her to the kitchen. Once there, Lucy poured them each a glass of apple juice from the fridge.

"I was sick last night, vomited most of the night and my stomach is really cramping. I don't know what's going on." Lucy gulped her juice down. She was so thirsty.

"That sounds awful. Can I call the doctor for you?"

"That's not necessary. I'll be okay. Probably just something I ate."

"You should go lie down. Claire, Gwen and I will manage Angela for the rest of the day. You need to take a break."

"Yeah, that's a great idea. I'd appreciate that." Lucy placed her empty glass down and leaned in to hug Cameron. As Cameron's arms automatically enfolded her, Lucy struggled against the need to pull her even closer. Her comforting embrace made Lucy melt into her. She could feel Cameron's heart beating frantically against her rib cage. Cameron's breath trailed down Lucy's neck, making her skin tingle. She tightened her arms around Cameron's neck, pulling her into her. Cameron strengthened her grip around Lucy's waist and her hands started traveling upward from her lower back, leaving a trail of butterflies as they moved. Lucy could feel Cameron move her face down toward hers and tangled her fingers into her soft hair. Time stood still. She opened her eyes and saw Cameron's face move into her, her mouth invitingly moving closer to hers.

"Coming through," Frankie announced.

Flushed, Lucy pulled away from Cameron's embrace and turned to Frankie. "Don't you have any other place to be? Surely my mom isn't your only client?" She bit her lip, regretting the words as they slipped out.

Frankie turned her attention to Cameron before looking at Lucy again. "I suggest you stop playing around and put your mother first. I'm sure you understand that she needs me."

115

Cameron looked at Lucy. "Frankie is a fantastic pharmacist. Your mom's needs could change in an instant and Frankie can organize meds quickly."

"Sure, whatever Mother needs. I'm going to lie down for a bit," Lucy mumbled before wiping her brow.

"Such a shame, are you not feeling well?" Frankie faked sympathy.

"I just didn't sleep well last night, is all," Lucy said.

"She was sick all night," Cameron offered. "Lucy, you should allow Frankie to help you, she has access to all the best pharmaceuticals."

"I might have some Imodium for you." Frankie inched closer to Lucy and felt her forehead. "Dude, you're like burnin' up."

"I appreciate your help, but I just need my bed. I'll be back by lunchtime," she said to Cameron.

"Of course, see you later," Cameron said.

"Laters," Frankie called with a broad grin on her face as Lucy left.

†

Back upstairs in her bedroom, Lucy dreaded another threatening note, and was relieved to find none. She dropped down onto her bed, not even bothering to cover herself with her duvet, and dozed off almost instantly.

Movement in her room woke her up, and she squinted her eyes, hoping, but also afraid of, catching her mystery stalker red-handed. It was Cameron. She sat next to her on the edge of her bed, holding a glass of liquid. Lucy lifted herself up on her elbows and looked at her.

"Some rehydration fluid for you." Cameron spoke softly as she handed her the glass.

Lucy took it from her and guzzled it down. Her throat was so dry, it felt like a tar road in Texas during a heat wave. Three gulps later she handed Cameron the empty glass. "What time is it?" she asked.

"It's five already. You never made it down for lunch. How are you feeling?" She felt her forehead with the back of her hand.

"Like crap. Thanks for the drink." She sat up in bed. "How's my mom?"

"Claire and Gwen looked after her well today. She's getting stronger and manages to turn herself now. I think your presence here is really helping her."

"I'm glad to hear that," Lucy said.

"I asked Connie to make you some chicken soup. Can I bring you some?"

"I'd love that. Will you sit with me, though?"

"Of course I'll sit with you. I was so worried about you, I haven't eaten yet either." With that, she got up and left the room.

Lucy lay back against her pillows and smiled at Cameron's remark on being concerned about her. It felt great having someone fussing over her. It was getting darker outside, and she could hear the rain slamming against the tiled roof. She struggled out of bed and went to shower and brush her teeth. Even though she had brushed her teeth that morning, all the vomiting from the night before, and then sleeping almost the entire day, had left her mouth and throat tasting horrible. She quickly dressed in a clean pair of nighties and walked back to her bed. And there, propped on her pillow, was another note. Lucy rushed to the doorway, hoping to catch her stalker in the act of sneaking away, but there was no one. Her gut told her it was Frankie. She knew it couldn't be Cameron, as she didn't seem like the type to try to hurt her. Lucy couldn't imagine it being any of the cleaning staff either. What would their reason be? Slowly, she opened the message.

I warned you, didn't I? Your illness was just a taste of what's to come.

Lucy felt sick to the pit of her stomach as she crawled back onto her bed, the note still in her hand. Moments later, Cameron came in with a tray. Without Cameron noticing, Lucy quickly stuck the piece of paper under her pillow. Cameron seemed oblivious to her flushed face as she placed the tray on the side table. Taking a bowl and a spoon, she handed Lucy the soup.

"Thanks," Lucy said as she carefully took the steaming bowl from her. "Where's Frankie?"

Cameron sat down next to Lucy, cautiously balancing her own soup. "She went out. Said she had a date with Dick."

"Oh? How long ago did she leave?"

"She left a little while ago. Right before I woke you, in fact."

Lucy frowned. Then Frankie could not have left the note, could she have? The note appeared while Lucy was in the bathroom, and if Frankie had left before Cameron had woken her, then someone else was leaving her these threatening notes. Unless Frankie had lied about going out, but then someone would have seen her around the house. Her chest ached at the thought that it could be Cameron. If it in fact was Cameron, then she was a damned good actor. Lucy scooped some soup into her spoon but was reluctant to eat and dropped it back into her bowl.

"Mmm, the soup's great," Cameron said after she took a bite. "You should really try eating some."

Lucy hesitated for a moment, and just as she wanted to risk a bite, she decided against it and put the bowl down. "Did you dish the soup?"

"I did. Why, is something wrong?"

"Would you mind if we swopped bowls?"

Cameron laughed. "That's a weird question. Why?" She leaned over and looked at the contents of Lucy's bowl. "Did I dish it wrong, or something?"

"Yours looks better than mine," she lied.

"Okay. Whatever floats your boat." Cameron passed her bowl to Lucy and took hers from her. "I've already had a bite, so you might get my germs," she joked.

119

Lucy watched as Cameron continued eating from her soup, the relief washing over her. She had her answer and she felt stupid for thinking Cameron was trying to poison her.

"What do you think of Dick?" Lucy asked.

Cameron swallowed her mouthful. "I'm not the biggest fan of dick, I prefer women."

"You know that's not what I meant…"

She smirked. "He seems like a nice guy. Why?"

"Just wondering."

"Eat," she said and watched as Lucy took a bite. "You need the nutrients."

"This is delicious. Please tell Connie thanks from me."

"How are you feeling? I'm really worried about you." She reached out and tucked a strand of stray hair behind Lucy's ear. "Careful. Don't eat your hair."

"I'm much better now." Lucy scooped soup onto her spoon and blew on it.

"You're so far away. Talk to me." Cameron's smile didn't reach her eyes.

Lucy shook her head and sighed. "How long do you think my mother has left? Have you spoken to the doctor lately?"

"He doesn't say much most of the time. The last time we discussed her progress, he said she wasn't looking too good. But like I've said before, I have noticed a change in her since your arrival. She seems… happier."

"You reckon?" Lucy mulled this over for a while. "I find that strange, seeing as I've been giving her such a hard time since I've arrived."

"She sometimes says your name in her sleep, you know."

"Must be having nightmares, then." Lucy swallowed hard.

"Nah. I think she missed you. I can see the love in her eyes when she looks at you." Cameron had finished her soup and watched Lucy as she ate.

She tilted her bowl to her lips and drained the contents before passing Cameron her empty dish. She took it from her and placed it on the tea tray.

"I can see the color returning to your cheeks. Scoot over," she said as she climbed in next to Lucy.

"I feel much better, thanks for dinner." Lucy leaned her head back and closed her eyes.

"I'm sorry you had a miscarriage at such a young age."

Lucy toyed with the tip of her nightdress. "It was a long time ago."

"I'm here if you need to talk…"

Just then her phone buzzed. She picked it up and looked at the screen before she exclaimed, "Paulie!" She pressed the answer button and placed it to her ear. "How's Paris? Are you pregnant yet?"

"I'm peeing on the stick as we speak. Lucy, I have never been so pampered in my life," his voice beamed from the earpiece.

Lucy felt Cameron tense beside her. "I'm so sorry," Lucy mouthed to her.

She stood and said, "I'll take the dishes down."

After Cameron had left, she returned her attention to her phone. Paul hadn't stopped talking and was chatting about all the clothes Alan had bought for him. She hadn't missed much of the conversation.

"Send me pictures," she said and laughed. It was good hearing his voice. She missed him. "When are you going home?"

"This weekend."

"Don't pout," Lucy teased.

"Not at all. Hey, we'll be landing in Cape Town. Please meet us at the airport. We can hang while we wait for our connecting flight to Durban."

"I would love that."

"I'll message you the flight details. Can't wait to see you," Paul said before ending the call.

Lucy smiled and stared at the ceiling for a moment. It would be so good to see him, even if it was only for a short while before they embarked on their flight home.

She remembered the note and placed it with the rest of them before returning to her bed. She heard her door open, and Cameron came back in.

"You done?"

"Yeah, sorry about that. It was my friend, Paulie. They're in Paris on vacation and they want me to see them this weekend when they return."

"I can take you," Cameron offered as she sat back down on Lucy's bed.

"You know I can drive, right?" she mocked.

"Just want to make sure you're safe," she said. "If you'd rather go alone, I'll stay."

"I'd actually love for you to meet them."

"Anyone of them a romantic interest?" Cameron raised an eyebrow.

Lucy snorted. "If you knew Paul and his husband you would not have to ask that question."

"Is Paul really ugly?" Cameron teased.

"Gay as they come," Lucy said with a grin. "Besides, I am not into men, remember?" She was sure she felt Cameron relax when she uttered the words. Was she jealous?

"Can't wait to meet them," she said.

Cameron moved and sat next to her again, to where she was before Paul had called. They sat for a while before Lucy spoke. "Hey, I'm sorry about all the drama with my mom and Frankie."

"You have your reasons," Cameron said and placed her arm around her shoulders.

Lucy leaned into her safe comfort. "Sucks that you're always in the middle of everything."

123

"I'm a big girl. I can handle it."

"Please don't leave."

Cameron shifted down. "Here, lie next to me. I'll take care of you," she muttered and pulled Lucy down to her. She put her arms around Lucy and drew her close.

"Sing me to sleep," Lucy said as she closed her eyes.

"Five little speckled frogs, sat on a speckled log, eating some most delicious bugs. Yum yum…."

Lucy giggled and closed her eyes.

†

When the morning light brightened her room, Lucy opened her eyes. Cameron was still there, snug behind her. As she tried to get up, Cameron groaned and tightened her grip. "Mm… No…"

Lucy relaxed into her embrace and enjoyed the heat radiating off her perfect body for a moment longer, but her bladder wasn't playing along. "I have to," she said as she hauled herself out of bed. She tiptoed to her bathroom and closed the door. Once inside, she quickly paid her tribute to Mother Nature and brushed her teeth. Her body felt relaxed, and she felt much better than the previous day. She rushed back to her room, hoping that Cameron would still be there, but when she opened her bathroom door, she found Cameron had already gone. "Damn," she muttered.

After she was dressed, she hurried down the stairs and checked in on her mother. Claire was there, feeding her breakfast. Lucy greeted them before she turned to leave the room, almost crashing into Cameron.

"Strong coffee, extra milk." She handed her a mug.

"Life saver," she said as she gratefully took the brew from her.

"I see you're feeling better today?" Cameron remarked, but it sounded more like a question.

"Much," Lucy said, raised herself onto her tippy toes and placed a kiss on Cameron's cheek. Cameron moved her face slightly toward Lucy, until their cheeks were touching. The sides of their lips made contact for a brief moment. Lucy exhaled and lowered her heels down to the ground.

Cameron groaned softly. "For that I'll make you coffee any time."

Lucy felt the heat reach her cheeks. "I love coffee," she said.

Later that day, Lucy was upstairs in her room when she gathered her threatening notes and sat on her bed. As she looked down at the first note, a drop of blood dripped down onto the paper. Her hand went up to her face. The blood was oozing out of her nose. She quickly dropped the messages back in her dresser drawer before she rushed to her bathroom, took a tissue from the bathroom counter, and pressed it against her nostrils. It was flowing, and she could feel a rush of panic fill her chest. As she squeezed, and leaned her head forward so the blood wouldn't run down her throat, everything went dark around her. Her legs gave way and the room disappeared around her.

†

"Lucy… Lucy!" She opened her eyes slowly. The light was too bright, and she squeezed her eyes shut. "Are you okay?" Cameron's voice rang in her ears as the room started reappearing around her. She must have passed out. She looked up at Cameron's worried face as she crouched over her.

"What time is it?" Lucy managed. Her throat was so dry, she could barely swallow.

"I don't know, it's probably almost dinner time." After pouring cool water into the basin, Cameron softly bathed Lucy's forehead, wiping away beads of sweat that had formed in her unconscious state. She cleaned off some of the drying blood and rinsed the face cloth.

"Shit. Where am I?" Lucy tried to sit, and almost lost her balance. She looked around herself. There was blood all over the floor. Her nose must have continued bleeding while she was passed out.

Cameron knelt and leaned her head against her chest. "On your bathroom floor. What the hell happened?" She stroked her matted hair.

The feel of Cameron's fingers on her scalp tingled beneath her gentle stroking. "I must have fainted."

"There's blood everywhere. Come, I'm taking you to the hospital."

"No. I'll be fine. Just a bit of Epistaxis." Lucy tried to stand, her head pounding. She closed her eyes, the room swaying around her.

"You lost a hell of a lot of blood. You need medical care." While still supporting her, Cameron stood and pulled her to her feet. She threw Lucy's right arm over her shoulder. "I'm taking you to the hospital. Kick and scream all you want." She gently supported Lucy against her, and cautiously guided her down the stairs.

Cameron helped Lucy into the Jeep and then got into the driver's seat. She swiftly started the engine and pulled away quickly. Cameron's grip tightened on the steering wheel as they sped through the city, heading toward the hospital. Lucy slumped in the passenger seat, her weakened body barely able to stay upright. The car ride felt like it was taking an eternity, each passing second reminding her of the pain and uncertainty that she was feeling.

As they arrived at the emergency entrance, Cameron parked the Jeep and rushed to open Lucy's door. With a gentle yet firm touch, she guided Lucy out and supported her weight as they entered the bustling hospital. The sterile smell of antiseptic filled the air, mixing with the sounds of beeping machines and hurried footsteps. Cameron helped Lucy into a cold, hard plastic chair and said, "Wait while I get a wheelchair."

A short moment later, Lucy saw her returning with a tall man who was pushing a wheelchair. They assisted Lucy into the chair and Cameron followed as the porter pushed her into one of the emergency unit cubicles. She felt dizzy and nauseous, wishing it all to end.

Once they were inside the cubicle, Lucy was lifted onto an examination bed and Cameron supported her and helped her lie down. She propped her head on a pillow and pulled a chair closer. Her hand reached for Lucy's and she felt Cameron's fingers close over hers.

"Good evening. I'm Dr. Johnson."

Lucy heard Cameron say, "Hi, Doctor."

Their voices sounded far away, and it felt to Lucy like she was drifting into a deep, dark tunnel. Her ears buzzed for a moment, then she continued listening to the voices in the distance. She closed her eyes while trying to listen to the conversation, and was grateful to have Cameron explain, as she simply couldn't even move her lips to speak.

"Yesterday she started vomiting…"

Lucy zoomed in and out as she heard Cameron tell Dr. Johnson her symptoms.

"Just a small prick," a nurse said who'd popped in out of nowhere. She noticed her arm was in a tourniquet. The nurse slipped a needle into her vein and first drew a few vials of blood, then connected an IV bag.

"I don't want to be admitted," Lucy said, her voice sounding desperate.

"Unfortunately, that's for the doctor to decide, love."

She sounded chirpy, and for a moment, Lucy wished she was on the other side of the IV line. She was far too weak to argue. "Where's my friend?" she asked the nurse before she slipped out.

"She's right outside, filling out the forms. Want me to call her for you?"

"No, it's fine. I'll wait till she's done."

"Good. My name's Beth. Call me if you need anything." She pulled the curtains shut behind her and whistled as she walked off.

Lucy could suddenly hear the hustle and bustle of the emergency unit. The familiar sound was welcoming to her ears. It dawned on her that she hadn't been admitted to hospital since she had the miscarriage fifteen years ago, and she realized what her previous patients must've felt like. She was feeling afraid and lonely. It felt like the hospital owned her, and she had lost all her rights as an independent human.

The curtains flew open again, and Cameron stepped in. "I see they've started you on the IV. That's fantastic. They're quickly testing your hemoglobulin levels—"

Lucy giggled. "You mean hemoglobin levels."

"That's what I said." She slapped Lucy playfully on the arm. "Be nice."

"I interrupted you. Sorry. What else did the doc say?" The IV fluids running through her veins made her feel better and more alert almost instantly.

"They're doing some blood tests. I can't believe you slept through the whole examination. Your blood pressure is very low, which he says is possible due to dehydration. That's why they put the drip up."

"I usually have a low blood pressure, so it's no biggie."

"I don't care how hard you argue. You're going to listen to the doctor and do whatever he tells you to do, you hear me?"

"Yes, *Mom*," Lucy teased.

"Can I get you anything from the soda machine?" She dug in her jean pocket and came up with a few coins.

"I don't think all that sugar and gas is going to be good for me right now. You go ahead, but hurry on back, okay?"

"I won't be long," she said before disappearing through the curtain.

Lucy closed her eyes for a few seconds before the curtains opened again. Dr. Johnson came in.

"How's my girl feeling?" He checked the IV bag and seemed satisfied with the amount left in the bag.

"I'm feeling a bit better, thanks, Doc."

"Your hb levels are a bit low, but it won't be necessary to do a blood transfusion. I'm just waiting for the rest of your lab results to return and if all's well, you can go home in the morning. I'll be back as soon as I hear from the lab. You rest in the meanwhile. Your body has taken quite a strain."

"Do we know what caused this?" she asked.

"Your friend told me you ate at a restaurant a few days ago, I'm gonna go with food poisoning for now. The nosebleed was probably brought on by stress."

"Thanks," Lucy said.

"Just a quick question, purely routine, have you taken any medication recently?"

"You mean drugs?" she asked.

"Drugs, medication, anything?"

"Nope. Only some vitamins a friend gave me." She froze. At least she had hoped that they were vitamins.

"No. Vitamins are perfectly safe. I'll be back shortly with your blood results."

She watched him slip through the curtains. Could Frankie be so evil? She knew she didn't like her, but up until now she hadn't been able to put a finger on it.

"Hey, you. What did your warden say?" Cameron was back.

"You got that right. I feel like a prisoner."

Cameron put her soda can down and sat on the chair next to Lucy before taking her hand and holding it tightly.

"He says I can go home tomorrow morning if my blood results are fine. I don't want to sleep here."

"How are you feeling? You're looking better."

"I'm feeling much better. The nausea is gone."

"Oh yes, they said they'd put something in the IV bag to help with that."

"Well, thank goodness, it's working."

There was a moment of silence as Cameron sipped from her cold drink.

"Hey, Cameron… Thank you for taking care of me."

She looked up at Lucy and squeezed her hand hard. "Any time."

Lucy watched the IV bag as the last bit of fluid dripped into her veins. To think that a whole liter of fluids had just been pumped into her body. She could feel herself getting stronger with each drop. The curtains opened again. Beth, the nurse, replaced the IV bag with a fresh one and said, "We're admitting you overnight. If your test results are okay, the doctor will discharge you in the morning."

"My mother needs me. I have to get home." Lucy attempted to sit.

"You're not going anywhere. Lay down and rest," Beth said in a firm tone.

Cameron patted Lucy's hand. "Remember I employed night staff for your mom? You have nothing to worry about."

It took a while for Cameron to assist with the documentation and once done, Lucy was taken to the ward. The doctor had prescribed her a sleeping tablet, so she assured Cameron that she was fine and that she should go home to get some sleep.

†

It was early the following morning that she was awoken by Dr. Johnson's friendly greeting. She opened her eyes and was relieved to see that Cameron had also entered the room. Cameron rushed to her side and kissed her forehead.

"Good morning, sunshine," she said.

"Test results look fine," Dr. Johnson offered in a gracious tone.

Beside her, Cameron gave a loud sigh of relief. "That's wonderful news," she said. "Can I take her home?"

Dr. Johnson nodded at Cameron and then turned to Lucy and said, "I'm happy to send you home. Drink lots of fluid and get plenty of rest. No undercooked chicken or raw fish for a while, and most of all, as I've mentioned, rest, rest, rest." The doctor removed her IV line, signed her charts, and left.

"Don't ever scare me like that again," Cameron said and sighed.

"Like I got sick on purpose." She clicked her tongue and sat up slowly.

Cameron helped her out of the hospital gown and passed her some clean clothes she had brought with her from home. While getting dressed, Lucy wondered if Cameron had seen the threatening notes in her dresser drawer while packing for her. After Lucy was dressed, Cameron held onto her all the way back to the car, and after helping her in, drove them home. The car ride back home was filled with a mixture of relief and quiet contemplation. Lucy stared out of the window, the city passing by in a blur, her mind still grappling with the events of the past day. Cameron glanced at her periodically, concern evident on her face.

When they finally arrived home, Cameron helped Lucy out of the car and guided her toward her room. "Did you manage to take a shower at the hospital?" Cameron asked once they reached Lucy's room.

"Nope. They gave me the sleeping tablet and I fell asleep immediately."

"Let's get you cleaned up."

Cameron supported her as she got into the bathroom. She then proceeded in helping her out of her clothes. Her hands brushed against Lucy's skin as she slipped her shirt over her head. Lucy's nipples went hard instantly. She held her breath as she seemed to have forgotten how to breathe. Cameron then lowered herself onto one knee and tucked the tips of her fingers under the elastic waistline of Lucy's sweatpants.

"If you're trying to propose, now is definitely not the time," Lucy commented with a hint of humor in her eyes.

Cameron smiled before sliding her sweatpants slowly down over her hips. Lucy stepped over them and watched as Cameron chucked them into the laundry basket. She then stood and helped Lucy into the shower before turning the water on. It was cold, so Lucy jumped back and leaned against her left arm, which wrapped around her uncovered waist. She watched Cameron's right hand as she adjusted the temperature. Goosebumps travelled all the way up Cameron's slender, yet muscular arm as the cold water hit it. When the water was warm enough, Lucy stepped into the spray.

Cameron took the soap and sponge, lathered it until it was white and foamy, and said, "Raise your arms."

Lucy knew she could probably wash herself, but felt a bit off-balance, so she obeyed.

Cameron soaped her skin in circular motions. She washed Lucy's legs, arms, back, neck and returned to her chest. Lucy inhaled sharply as she moved the sponge over her nipples. She swallowed hard. Cameron's hand travelled down to Lucy's lower body parts, so Lucy stopped her and took the sponge from her.

"I can wash there," she said, her voice sounding strange to her own ears. Lucy quickly cleaned herself and dropped the sponge to the floor as she rinsed.

Cameron had the shampoo ready by the time Lucy had finished, and she allowed her to help her with her hair. Cameron's fingertips gently scrubbed her scalp, sending goosebumps all the way down her body.

"You'd make an excellent nurse," she said when Cameron was done with her hair. Lucy closed her eyes and allowed the water to wash over her, enjoying the heat massaging her skin. When she opened her eyes again, Cameron stood holding a towel.

"Let's get you dried and dressed." Cameron reached in and switched off the water. She wrapped the soft material around Lucy and helped her out of the shower.

"Need to brush my teeth," she said and started for the basin.

Cameron stood behind her, supporting her as she leaned over the sink, cleaning her teeth. Once she was done, Cameron walked her to her bed, making sure she didn't lose her balance.

When she was safely seated, Cameron went to her closet and took some clean clothes from the shelves. She handed Lucy a T-shirt and assisted her while she put it on. She then helped Lucy into clean panties and a clean pair of sweatpants.

As soon as she was dressed, Cameron took her to the family room. She helped her get comfortable on the sofa and handed her the remote. "Put your feet up, watch some TV and be a slob. That's an order."

"Thanks." Lucy smiled at her. "You've been really great."

"I'm going to Connie in the kitchen to see what she's making. You must be hungry."

"Could you also please check on my mom?"

"Of course," she said and left.

136

While flicking through the channels, Lucy thought of the threatening notes and the vitamins that Frankie had given her. She could quite easily have replaced them with something else. What type of a person could be devious enough to poison another person?

"Connie made you some pasta." Cameron's voice brought her mind back to reality. She walked in carrying a large tray with plates and glasses of juice. Lucy looked at the food when she placed the tray down on the coffee table in front of her. The spaghetti looked fantastic.

"This looks divine," Lucy said. "Thank you."

"You're welcome," Cameron said. "Can I grate you some cheddar cheese?"

"Yes. You can never have enough cheese."

Lucy watched in amazement as Cameron grated almost half the block of cheese over her food.

"Here you go." She handed Lucy the plate and a fork. "One 'yellow' meal coming up."

Lucy smiled as she took the plate that was mostly cheese. "Thanks," she said before taking a huge bite and chewing the food. The warm and flavorful spaghetti coated Lucy's taste buds, and the melting cheddar cheese added a delightful richness to the dish. She savored her mouthful, enjoying the perfect blend of textures and flavors. As she chewed, Lucy couldn't help but show her appreciation with an enthusiastic smile.

Cameron chuckled as she watched Lucy indulge in her cheesy meal. "I'm glad you like it," she said. "Cheese makes everything better, doesn't it?"

Lucy nodded, still chewing. "Absolutely. Cheese has a magical way of enhancing any dish."

Cameron sat down next to Lucy, picking up her own plate of pasta. "Connie has always been a master in the kitchen."

Lucy nodded, taking another bite. "This is delicious." While she ate from her plate, her thoughts drifted to the letters. "I need to talk to you," she finally said to Cameron after she swallowed a mouthful. "And I need you to keep an open mind," she added with a low tone.

Cameron hesitated for a moment. "O...kay? Sounds serious." She frowned as she popped her full fork into her mouth.

"I've been receiving threatening notes," Lucy said with hesitation in her voice, all the while watching Cameron's reaction.

Her face was expressionless. "What do you mean?"

"I mean, someone's been dropping threatening notes in my room for me to find."

Cameron frowned. She dropped her fork onto her plate and stared at Lucy. "Here? Threatening notes? What do you mean?"

"The first one said that I must go home or suffer the consequences. The second one said that I had been warned and now was the time for our final game, and the third one said my illness was just a taste of what was to come."

Cameron's face went red and she looked livid. "Please tell me you're joking?"

"I wish I was, Cameron."

"When did you get these?" Her facial expression was that of complete shock.

"They started soon after I arrived."

"And you're only telling me this *now*? Lucy, we have to get these to the police. They sound like serious threats. This could be the reason why you've been sick. Do you think someone's been poisoning you?"

"Here's the thing... Frankie gave me vitamins, which I started taking two days ago, and I became sick that very same evening after we went to breakfast."

"I've known Frankie for quite some time now, and I can't imagine that she would be evil enough. She can be annoying, that much I can agree with, but she's not devious."

"I got my last letter the night before last night, while Frankie was out with Dick. This really baffles me."

"See? There's no way it could be her. Where are they? I need to see them."

"I'll show you," Lucy said. "Right after we've eaten."

"This is serious, Lucy. Please don't let this slide. You can leave it to me, I can take care of it for you. I'll call the police. Tell me where they are, I'll go fetch them." She put her plate of half-eaten food down.

139

"They're in my dresser drawer."

Cameron shot up and left the room. A few minutes later she returned looking baffled. "Which dresser? I looked everywhere. There was nothing."

Lucy sighed and rolled her eyes. "Women," she said jokingly. "Help me up." She reached for Cameron's hand and stood.

"You okay to climb the stairs to your room?"

"I'm feeling much better."

With Cameron's support, they mounted the stairs. When they reached her door, Cameron opened it and proceeded ahead of her. Once inside, she stopped and faced Lucy.

Lucy walked past Cameron and went to her bedside table. "Here." She picked up the vitamins and handed them to Cameron. "Can we take these to the laboratory and have them tested? I don't want to insinuate anything, but rather safe than sorry."

She took the bottle from her, opened the lid and sniffed. "They smell like normal vitamins," she said. "I know someone at the lab who can analyze them discreetly."

"Can we take them now?"

"No, *we* can't take them, but I will. You must rest. Doctor's orders, remember? Can I see the notes?"

Lucy went over to her dresser, opened the drawer and looked inside. The blood instantly drained from her face when she saw that it was empty. The papers were all gone.

She looked at Cameron desperately and was sure that Cameron could see the shock in her face. "They're not here anymore." Her voice was trembling, and her legs felt weak. Whoever had left them for her had snuck into her room and taken all her proof.

"Gone?" Cameron came closer and inspected the drawer. "That's where I looked."

"You must be thinking I've completely lost my mind. I promise you I haven't. They were in here last night. I distinctly remember my nose bleeding on them." She went over to her bed and sank down onto it.

Cameron followed her and sat beside her. "Hey." She raised an arm and pulled Lucy closer to her. "I believe you."

Lucy leaned her head on Cameron's shoulder and closed her eyes. Her familiar fragrance filled Lucy's senses and she wished she could stay in her arms forever. She made her feel so safe.

A short moment later Cameron spoke. "I'm going to take your vitamins to the lab." She placed her arms around Lucy for a quick hug. "Just look after yourself while I'm gone. I won't be long. Lock your door and don't let anyone in."

"Thanks for the concern, but I'd rather watch TV. I have Olaf, Robert, the gardener, Connie, Claire, and Gwen in case I need anything. Oh, and… Frankie, I guess."

"Of course," she agreed and mulled it over for a while. "Wow, it could be almost anyone, you know?"

"I know."

"Lucy, I just want you to know. It wasn't me. I don't know why it's so important to me that you know this, but I really hope you believe me."

She nodded. "I trust you, Cameron."

Cameron escorted Lucy back to the TV room and watched her get comfortable on the couch before she left. Lucy hoped she had done the right thing by telling her about the notes and trusting her with the vitamins. Lucy clicked the remote and chose a comedy, and after a while Connie brought her some tea and freshly cut fruit salad.

"Connie," Lucy called to her before she left.

"Yes, Lucy?" Connie turned around and faced her. She was a short elderly lady. Lucy had known her most of her life. She had cooked for her parents even when Lucy was a child, but even so, Lucy realized she didn't know her well. She felt guilty for never putting in much effort with the staff. She guessed she was as much of a snob as her parents were.

"Is there anyone on the staff that doesn't seem all that trustworthy? Claire? Gwen?"

Connie looked confused for a minute. "No. Not that I know of. Why?"

"Just wondering. Okay. Thanks. Feel free to come join me if you want to watch a movie."

"Okay. Thanks." She looked uncomfortable for a moment but smiled before she left.

After watching the comedy, Lucy sighed and wondered what to do next. She was bored and Cameron was taking forever to get home.

She wondered where Frankie was, so she took a stroll around the house. She knew that Frankie occupied a room on the first floor, at the end of the passage just a few doors down from Cameron's room. Maybe if she searched her room, Lucy would find the notes that she most probably had taken. After climbing the stairs to the first floor, she walked down the passage slowly, and when she reached Frankie's door, Lucy was disappointed to see that it was closed. She stood and listened for a while, and when she couldn't hear any movement from within, she knocked. Softly at first, but when there was no response, she opened the door and quickly slipped inside.

If Frankie wasn't in her room, where the hell else could she be? Lucy went over to her window and looked outside. There was nobody in the garden except for the gardener that was pruning the trees. Rushing over to her dressing table, Lucy searched through the drawers quickly. There was nothing but the usual stuff women kept in their makeup drawers. Then she searched the bedside table, and the only thing she found there was an engagement ring. Lucy lifted it toward the light and admired the clarity of the diamond. She quickly returned it to the drawer and continued her search. Except for the ring, she couldn't find anything out of place.

But the ring could have belonged to someone else for all she knew, so it most probably didn't mean anything.

The sound of footsteps made her want to lose consciousness as fear overtook her, and she could have jumped out the window had it not been for her fear of falling and surviving with a broken back. Lucy jumped into the shower and closed the lush shower curtain. Just then, Frankie came bustling into her room, and as Lucy tried to steady her breathing, she glimpsed Frankie through the small gap where the shower curtain didn't reach the wall. Lucy could see straight into her bedroom via the reflection in the large bathroom mirror. Frankie dropped a whole bunch of shopping bags onto her bed. Then she smiled as she undressed quickly, and donned a new dress she must have just purchased. She walked into the bathroom, admiring her reflection in the mirror, turning around and giggling happily. Lucy moved back slowly and quietly, hoping that Frankie couldn't see her behind the shower curtain. Her eyes shot wide when she heard Frankie mutter, "See if you can resist me now, Cameron."

It took all of Lucy's willpower not to charge at her through the shower curtain like in the movie *Psycho*, and she clenched her fists at her side while she waited for Frankie to try on the rest of her dresses. The next thing she heard was Frankie leaving the room and closing the door behind her. Lucy waited a few minutes, and then slipped out slowly before rushing up to her bedroom. Once inside, she dropped onto her bed, and lay there thinking of what she had just done. Her heart was still racing, and her head was spinning.

A little while later, Cameron knocked and entered her room. She sat next to Lucy on her bed and patted her arm. Lucy looked up at her and waited in anticipation for the results. "The toxicology report came back all clear. Lucy, those vitamins were just that. Vitamins. Nothing odd there." Cameron spoke softly.

"The pills could have been switched by the person who came to fetch the notes," Lucy insisted.

"I know, but there's not much we can do about that now. How are you feeling?" she asked.

"I'm like new. Been walking around a little. How's my mom?"

"Don't stress about her today, you're exhausted. Claire and Gwen will manage. I'll drop in every now and then."

Lucy started to sit up, "I really should go down to her."

"I'll get her out of bed, and I'll make sure she's strapped in and safe. You just stay here or go back downstairs and lay on the couch. I'll bring your laptop down if you want it."

"It's cool. I'm just going to stay in my room for a while."

After Cameron left, Lucy sat on her bed and thought everything through. First it was the whispering in her mother's room, then the notes, and then her unexplainable illness. It couldn't be Cameron, because she just didn't fit the bill. Lucy was now more convinced than ever that it was Frankie. She was jealous, because she wanted Cameron to herself, and getting rid of Lucy somehow made sense. But one had to be psycho playing with people's lives just to get a date.

Lucy thought it over for a while, and then walked over to her window. She was feeling better, not so dizzy anymore, and she wanted to get moving a bit. She was sick of being cooped up inside the house all day. As she looked down at the garden from her window, she saw Cameron pushing her mother to their spot at the cliff-edge, and her heart skipped a few beats. Her feelings for Cameron seemed to intensify by the minute. She seemed like such a caring, kind person. Every cell in Lucy's body wanted to be close to her. As she watched Cameron walk with her mother, her heart swelled ten sizes, but that soon evaporated when she spotted Frankie scurrying after them, trying to catch up—in her new dress. The dress was white, short, and even from her bedroom window, Lucy could see her cleavage. What a cheap move. Lucy just couldn't stand there and watch this happen.

As much as she wanted to run, she did not want to overreact, so she walked toward the edge of the property, where they sat side by side right there on Lucy's rock. Her annoyance doubled with every step, especially when she saw Frankie look at Cameron sideways and laugh. Lucy knew she was being jealous and that she had no right to be, but there was nothing she could do to be at ease about Frankie openly flirting with Cameron. She slowed her pace when she got closer, so that showing up out of the blue wouldn't make her appear too obvious.

"Hey, Mom," she greeted Angela, who in turn looked up at her.

"Hello, Lucy."

Frankie's head spun around, and she looked at Lucy in dismay, and so did Cameron, but Cameron's disapproval was for other reasons. "I told you to rest, and so did the doctor. What are you doing up and about? Geez, nurses really do make the worst patients."

"I am sick and tired of my room—"

"Then go lie on the couch, I told you I'd bring you whatever you needed."

Lucy's mother looked confused. "Is she ill?" Her eyes flashed to Lucy, filled with concern.

"She had a stomach bug and then nosebleeds. I took her to the hospital yesterday. She was kept overnight, and the doctor this morning said she must rest."

Angela looked at Lucy, her eyes strict, the way Lucy remembered them when she was much younger. "Go now, off to bed with you."

Cameron stood. "Come, I'll go with you."

"What about my mother? We can't leave her here."

Angela shook her head in dismay. "Go. I'm not a child. Frankie can call Claire for me."

"She's not wrong," Cameron reassured her and placed her hand on the small of Lucy's back.

"Babe, she's a grown woman. She can take care of herself." Frankie's voice had a nervous twitch.

"Oh, Frankie. Stop this nonsense," Angela said with a loud tone. "Cameron, help my stubborn daughter."

Frankie rolled her eyes like a teenager and sighed.

†

Cameron led Lucy through her own bedroom door. "You can stay in my room for a while, it'll be a good change of scenery." With her hand still resting on Lucy's lower back, she walked her over to her bed. She turned to face Lucy and rested both of her hands on her hips. "Does that suit you?"

Lucy could feel her thumbs weakly gripping onto her hip bones, giving her a tremble in her breath. The thumping of her heart withheld her courage to look Cameron in the eye, so she locked them to her neck. She placed both of her hands on the bumps of Cameron's shoulders, and slid them down to her upper arms, watching as her pulse started visibly showing under her jaw, in the base of her throat.

"I think..." She paused for a moment while she slid her hands back up to Cameron's shoulders, and lifted her gaze to Cameron's eyes. "This will do just fine."

Cameron took a deep breath, as if she had been holding it in while waiting for her response. The sound of struggle in Cameron's lungs made Lucy's lower lip drop. She traced her fingers along the muscles on her shoulders and up to her long, slender neck. Cameron's face lowered closer to hers, and as the small hairs on their faces were tickling against each other, she could feel Cameron's warm shaking breath leak down the sensitive skin on the side of her neck. She breathed quietly into Cameron's ear and along her cheek, taking slow movements until their noses touched. Cameron flinched and pulled her face slightly away from hers, but when she didn't move away, Cameron softened and put her nose back against Lucy's. The sound of their breathing increased. Lucy was drowning in the pounding of her heartbeat. Her stomach twisted with hunger for Cameron. The air separating them felt static, but Cameron took a deep breath before pulling herself back.

"You really need to rest. I'm not telling you again." She placed her right hand on Lucy's shoulder and lightly pushed her down until she was seated on Cameron's bed. Lucy placed her hand over Cameron's and looked up at her. Cameron looked so confident towering over her body. The darkness of Cameron's bedroom gave a sensual complement to her feminine features. Lucy traced her fingers from Cameron's hand, up her arm and felt her stomach clench as Cameron shivered. Cameron's breathing increased as her thumb picked at the strap of Lucy's tank top and pulled it closer to the edge of her shoulder, but she stopped herself and dropped to her knees in front of Lucy. She placed both of her hands on the sides of Lucy's thighs with her eyes locked to her lips. Cameron swallowed, and with her eyes still locked on her mouth she said under her breath, "Lucy, you really need to—"

"Rest?" she interrupted.

Cameron looked up from Lucy's lips to her eyes and backed away before she stood. "Yes. You're safe here. I will always keep you safe." She held onto Lucy's cheek with her right hand, bent down and lightly kissed the top of her head before walking out, closing the door behind her.

Lucy sat on Cameron's bed, alone in her room, with an uncomfortable craving for her. She looked around for a while, trying to catch her breath. Cameron's king-sized bed was layered in grey and white linen. Her walls were painted in a light clay-colored tint. Lucy eased her body down until her head rested into the plush pillows. Cameron's delicious smell still lingered in the air. Turning her head and pushing her face into Cameron's pillow, she inhaled her scent. It smelled so good, she wanted to be surrounded by her fragrance. The realization dawned on her that she was in Cameron's bed. This was where she slept. Where every part of her body had touched. It made Lucy quiver. She slid her hands under the duvet and writhed her body around over the bed. This was the most erotic, intense feeling she had ever experienced. Knowing that Cameron had been there, slept there… most probably even touched herself there.

She closed her eyes, imagining Cameron touching herself. Was she thinking of Lucy when she did that? Her fingers gripped the blankets and pulled them around her. She rolled over the hill that the bedding had formed and pulled the duvet over her. The feel of the material on her skin made every cell tingle. Cameron's presence surrounded her. Her remaining aura penetrated her. Lucy was in heaven. Cameron was the most titillating woman she had ever met. She wanted more of her. All of her. She wondered what she tasted like. What her lips would feel like. How her tongue would feel.

A soft knock on the door brought her senses back to reality. Before she managed to answer, the door opened. Cameron stood there for a brief moment, looking with amusement at Lucy entangled in her bedding before entering and closing the door softly behind her.

"Your mom's back in bed and comfortable," she said before walking over to Lucy and laying down beside her. "Thought I'd keep you company." Cameron lay on her right side, facing Lucy, her head propped up on a pillow. Cameron's left hand reached for Lucy's and she exhaled shakily when their fingers met. "Don't move," she whispered. Cameron made slow circle movements with her fingertips, up her arm until her hand reached Lucy's shoulder, then moved slowly over her collarbone and teased its way down, between her breasts all the way to her belly button. "Close your eyes and relax."

Lucy's heart knocked against her ribs, pumping up to her throat. She obeyed and closed her eyes.

"Breathe," Cameron commanded as her fingers stroked up and down Lucy's belly at an excruciatingly slow pace. As soon as Cameron's fingers reached the underside of Lucy's breast, she moved them down again until they reached her hipbone.

Lucy sucked the air in and shakily let it out. Trying hard to relax.

Up and down, Cameron's hand went. Never once touching her breast, nor travelling down past her pelvic area. The slow tease had Lucy breathing heavily, as she was trying to keep up with her increasing heartbeat. She realized that she had started moving her hips in slow motion, to the same pace as Cameron's hand. With every movement, her hand went slightly lower, almost touching where Lucy so badly longed for her to go. As Cameron's hand slid down, Lucy moved her pelvis up, aching for her to move lower. Cameron shifted her hand up again and as Lucy thought Cameron might touch her breast, she moved it back down again. Up again, and this time Cameron's fingertips almost brushed against her left nipple. She stifled a moan and restrained herself, so as to not grab Cameron.

"Do you want me to touch you?" Cameron's voice was low, her breath in Lucy's ear causing goosebumps down her body.

"Yes. Please..." she begged.

Cameron's fingers travelled up and playfully tickled her left nipple, then down again, this time reaching her pulsing bud. She arched her hips upward, only for Cameron's touch to go back up again, leaving Lucy aching for more. She reached her right nipple this time, gently grazing it before tracing her hand back down again. This time she slid her fingers over Lucy's clit, at an excruciatingly slow pace. Her touch was gentle and barely brushed against her, causing Lucy's need to grow beyond what she could tolerate. Her body tensed, wanting more. Cameron didn't budge. Her fingers were gone again, moving up to her left nipple. And back down again, where she thrust her hips to meet Cameron. Her hand moved upward again.

"Stop tormenting me... I need you... Please..." She reached for Cameron's hand, trying to pull it back down, but Cameron resisted her desperation.

"Relax. I've got you," she said, tickled her nipple for a moment and then back down again, caressing between her legs. Lucy parted them, welcoming the release. Cameron stroked gently, not moving away.

Lucy moved her hips, meeting the rhythm of Cameron's stroking. "Oh, god, Cameron, I'm so close. Please don't stop..."

Cameron applied a little more pressure, which caused Lucy to erupt. She gasped, held her breath and gripped the sheets.

Her hips pushed up against Cameron's hand. "Yes. Yes. Oh yes," she hissed.

Cameron continued her caresses until Lucy backed down and relaxed into the bed.

Lucy turned and reached for Cameron, wanting to touch her, to feel more of her, but Cameron caught her by the wrist and gently pulled her away. "No. This was about you. Now you'll rest."

"Please let me touch you," Lucy pleaded.

"You have no idea how badly I want you right now," she said in a low tone.

"Then allow me to…"

She grinned. "Turn on your side. Let me hold you."

Lucy obeyed and turned onto her right side.

Cameron wrapped her arm around Lucy and held onto her tightly. Lucy could hear the trembling in Cameron's breathing and felt her body shiver behind her. She knew Cameron needed her too and it made her smile. She closed her eyes and soon drifted off. When she woke, Cameron was gone.

†

Lucy went downstairs to the kitchen and set about making a pot of coffee. She had slept for about two hours and could use some caffeine to clear her head. As she pushed the plunger down, she heard footsteps entering the kitchen behind her.

"Hey there, you." Cameron took two large mugs off the shelf, the jug of milk from the fridge, and then came over and stood right next to her. Her sudden closeness had caught Lucy completely off guard, and she had to take a sharp intake of breath in order to keep herself steady. The memory of what Cameron had done to her earlier made her flush.

"How are you feeling?"

"Fit as a fiddle. Thank you for helping me... uh... rest."

"I left when you were asleep. Didn't want to bother you. Glad you're feeling better."

After she poured the coffee, Cameron added the milk. They took their mugs and sat down by the table.

"Your mom is worried about you. Let's finish our coffees and go show her that you're still alive," Cameron said.

Lucy drank while watching Cameron's movements. She was so comfortable in her own skin, it amazed her. Cameron didn't make her feel awkward that she had just watched Lucy at her most vulnerable. Instead, she continued as if nothing had transpired in her room earlier. This put Lucy at ease. It was good to feel innocent and normal. She

155

downed the rest of her coffee and watched Cameron do the same.

"Shall we go?" Cameron asked and stood.

Lucy followed Cameron as she led the way to her mother's bedroom.

Angela was awake and attempting to brush her own hair. When she spotted Lucy, her face lit up. "There you are. How do you feel? Did you have a nice nap?"

Lucy blushed, remembering what had helped her relax. "I did and I feel fabulous."

"That's good to hear. Come. Sit with me for a while." She reached her hand out as if to pull Lucy toward her.

"Okay." Lucy shifted the chair closer and sat next to Angela's bed.

"Thank you," she said softly. "I just want to have you near me for a bit."

Lucy looked into her pale blue eyes, noticing they glistened with unshed tears. She reached up and took her mother's hand.

"I'm so sorry…" Her voice trailed off as she spoke. "I am so…so sorry," she said and coughed.

"I know." Lucy struggled to swallow.

"Do you want me to leave?" Cameron asked.

"No. You can stay," Lucy said.

Cameron walked over to the other side of Angela's bed and occupied a chair.

"I missed you… so much." Angela spoke in a weak voice. She sounded tired.

"You did?"

"I did. I made so many mistakes, and this… illness… is my punishment. I am so very sorry, Sausage."

Lucy smiled at the endearment. She hadn't called her "Sausage" since Lucy was about seven.

"I was wrong… So wrong…"

"It's okay, Mom. Don't talk about it." Lucy sniffed as she held onto her hand tightly.

"Allow love to enter your heart…" she managed, but Lucy could tell it was exhausting for her to talk. She pointed at Lucy's chest with her fingers. "Love is the most important thing."

"I'll try, Mom."

"No… Don't just try. Love is everything… You have been pushing people away for far too long…." She breathed heavily now and started coughing again. "Love… Cameron…" Cough.

"No, Mom, this is Lucy. Not Cameron."

"Lucy… I know…" She sighed.

"I'm sorry. I don't really understand. You love Cameron?"

"You… love Cameron…" She coughed again.

Lucy looked over at Cameron who looked pensive.

"Mom, I think you're a bit confused," Lucy tried.

"I love you… Always… have…"

"I love you too, Mom."

Angela held onto Lucy's hand until she drifted off to sleep. Lucy pressed the morphine pump's button once, to make sure she was pain-free for a while at least. "Shall we leave her now and let her sleep?" Lucy spoke quietly to Cameron.

"Yeah. Let's do that." Cameron got up, walked over to Lucy and took her hand before leading her out of the room, closing the door behind them.

Once outside the room, Cameron looked serious. "We need to talk," she said.

Lucy's stomach twisted. "Sure," she said and followed her back to the kitchen.

Cameron poured two more cups of coffee, handed her one, and motioned for her to sit.

She sat. "Shit's getting serious," she tried to joke, but Cameron didn't smile.

Cameron sank down on the chair beside her. "I haven't been completely honest with you." She swallowed hard.

Lucy stared at her. Something told her she wasn't going to like what Cameron had to say, and she hoped—wished—so hard that it had nothing to do with her threatening messages. Her eyes went wide. "Talk."

"The reason why I emailed you was not to come and be your mother's nurse."

"Oh?" Now she was confused. The conversation took a different direction than what Lucy had expected.

"Look. This is difficult, so I'm just going to get to the point. Your mother asked me to kill her…"

"Wait. What?" Lucy felt her face heat up.

Cameron leaned over the table and put her face in her hands. "She wanted me to overdose her on morphine. I couldn't do it. She was the closest thing to a mother I had ever had. After I started working for her, I really bonded with her, I love her. I just couldn't do it. I'm so sorry." She wiped her hands over her face and looked at Lucy.

"Carry on." Lucy was completely confused.

"I told her I couldn't do it, that's why she told me to email you. She told me you'd do it. Only, once I had met you and gotten to know you, I didn't know how to tell you. Your mother told me you hated her, and you could do it."

Lucy thought back to their hushed conversation the other day in her mother's room. At least that part started making sense. But where did the threats come from? "Carry on."

"Frankie would provide the drugs, chart the dosages incorrectly, so that no questions would be asked after your mother died. Your mother has offered her a great deal of money for her co-operation."

Lucy felt numb.

"The doctor was in on it, too. He would document the death as natural causes. So, no questions would be asked, and your mother could still have her wish. And… whoever killed her wouldn't go to prison for murder."

"She's paying the doctor, too?"

"Handsomely."

This whole scam had been pre-organized, only no one had the guts to push the syringe. It had absolutely nothing to do with the threats, but at least some of the secrecy was starting to make sense.

"I can't believe this." Lucy choked back tears. "You know I can't do this, don't you?"

"Yes, I know." Cameron sighed. "I told them that the other day. Frankie was convinced you would, you just needed to trust me first, and then you'd fulfill your mother's wishes."

Lucy touched Cameron's arm lightly. She was angry but appreciated her honesty. "So my mom asked for me, not because she missed me, but because she wanted me to *kill* her?"

Cameron shook her head. "Lucy, you have no idea how much pain your mom has been in, but since you've been back, she is a different person. I could see her slowly coming back to life. She did miss you. That part was true. She never told me why you guys weren't on speaking terms, which was why I was so angry at you when we met. I always thought you were just a brat, not wanting anything to do with your family. But after you spoke to your mom about your miscarriage, things started making sense." She cleared her throat. "She really did call your name in her sleep."

"I'm glad you told me. But I can't do it."

"That's the thing. Since you've been here, she's been doing well. She's not in that much pain anymore. You really know your business."

Lucy smiled at the compliment. "I'm glad I could make a difference."

"And I'm relieved you and your mom are finally on speaking terms."

"I never thought that would ever happen." Lucy leaned back and crossed her arms over her chest.

"It's been quite a journey," Cameron mused.

CHAPTER SIX

Paul's face was covered in hair when he strolled through the *Arrivals* sliding doors, pushing his trolley which was stacked to the top with all his pink luggage. Alan walked beside him, smiling broadly when they spotted Lucy.

"Juicy Lucy!" Paul exclaimed and pounced to hug her. "Oh, how I have missed you, my sweetie."

"What's with the big-ass beard, girlfriend?" Lucy wrapped her arms around him and held onto him as hard as her arms could hold. She pulled away and hugged Alan. "Good to see you guys," she said to him.

"He didn't shave anywhere this vacation, because he said he wants to be a bear."

Lucy laughed and introduced them to Cameron. Paul's eyes lit up, and as Cameron stretched out her hand to greet him, Paul wrapped himself around Cameron. "What handshakes are you trying to give? We're practically family."

Cameron grinned and hugged them both.

Paul put his arm over Lucy's shoulder and winked at Cameron. "Lead the way, gorgeous," he said to Cameron. "Take us to a watering hole so we can wet our throats."

Lucy reached up and stroked Paul's beard. "Can I buy you a razor?"

"Weed eater more like," Alan said and laughed. "But it's super sexy, isn't it?"

"Incredibly sexy," Cameron joked. "Just want to rub up against it."

"Oooh. Don't be a tease," Paul said and slapped Cameron's arm.

With the help of Alan's frequent flier miles, they had access to the slow lounge. Alan led the way to a table, and they all sat down and ordered drinks.

"Where on earth did you find this delicious, juicy piece of meat, Lucy?" Paul asked, referring to Cameron. "She's so gorgeous, I wish I wasn't gay."

"You always want what you can't have," Alan said to Paul. "I'm sure Cameron prefers her 'snacks' less hairy."

Cameron chuckled. "I'm a firm believer of not knocking it till you've tried it."

"Don't behave, baby. See where it gets you," Paul immediately responded.

"Would you ladies like to get a room?" Lucy chimed in.

"I'll pay for it," Cameron said and mockingly pulled out her wallet.

"This is a naughty one, Lucy. She's a keeper."

"Oh, we're not—" Lucy started to object, but was interrupted by the waiter who had brought their drinks and placed them down.

"So? How was it?" Lucy asked as she picked up her drink.

"We had the most beautiful view of the Eiffel tower," Alan started.

Paul grinned and poked Alan's cheek. "I had a better view of your Eiffel tower."

Cameron spoke in a French accent. "City of romance."

Paul growled, "Grrr…"

Alan slapped him on his knee and added, "Oh boy, the transitioning to bear is finally happening. Save some for later."

"Lucy, the men there were," Paul kissed his fingertips and groaned, "*magnifique.*"

Alan nodded exaggeratedly and agreed. "Right? We wanted to jump their bone…z. Unfortunately, you know, the ball and chain…"

Paul gasped. "*Un*fortunately?"

"I kid, I kid. You're the only man I want," Alan said.

"I'm sure you guys were still the hottest boys there," Cameron said, smiling broadly.

"Well, *duh*," Paul said and laughed. He added in a soft tone, "Thank you, pookie."

Cameron jokingly blew Paul a kiss.

"So, Lucy, give us the juicy. What's happening at your mom's?"

Lucy gave a quick explanation of her mother's condition. Alan asked a few medically related questions which Lucy answered.

They then discussed Paul and Alan's trip to Paris, but sadly the time went by so fast that it felt like only a few minutes before it was time for them to catch their connecting flight. After they said their goodbyes, Cameron and Lucy went back to their car.

Lucy beamed. "It was so nice to see them again. Gosh, I missed them."

"They're such awesome guys. Glad I came with." Cameron looked over at her. "Good to see you so happy."

"Thank you for coming with."

†

Once back at home, Lucy went up to her room. She rummaged through her closet for something nice to wear. Seeing Paul had stirred the nostalgia that she had been suppressing. She really wanted to go home, but on the other side she couldn't imagine her life without Cameron. Since she had entered her life, Lucy's whole perspective of her future had changed. Also, being back in her childhood home felt good. She looked at the clothes that she had gathered and sighed. She really needed to go purchase a whole new wardrobe, and getting out on her own would be refreshing.

After she gathered her tote bag, she went searching for Cameron and spotted her on the sofa in the lounge, reading a book. "I'm going shopping," she announced in a chirpy voice.

Cameron slammed her book shut and placed it on the coffee table. "Where are we going?" she asked.

"We? You're such a doll, but I'm sure you can manage the fort without me for a while. I'd like to go by myself, if you don't mind?"

"I see. Okay." She picked her book back up again and searched for her page.

"Need anything?"

"Since you're buying, Gummy Bears."

Lucy grinned and nodded. "Gummy Bears it is."

Lucy entered the large garage that adjoined the kitchen area and gasped as she saw all the cars parked in the gigantic showroom. It was no wonder Olaf was still working there after all these years. She counted a total of twelve sports cars. Dangling from the wall to her left, she saw all the keys, marked clearly. After taking the one that said Volante, she pressed the button and listened to where the beeping sound came from.

Lucy whistled as she clambered into the green convertible Aston Martin Volante, which probably used to be part of her dad's collection. As the engine roared to life, her chest tightened with pure excitement. She pulled out of the garage, slowly at first, making sure she got the hang of the steering wheel and how it drove. By the time she reached the second corner, she couldn't contain herself. As she pressed her foot down on the gas pedal, the force pushed her back into the seat. The wind whipped her hair and she felt invincible. She knew she was driving too fast, but she couldn't resist. Soon after she hit the open road, she noticed a van following her, really trying hard to keep up with her speed. She shrugged off the negative feeling because when she reached the mall a few minutes later, she was the only vehicle on the road.

She visited every clothing store at the mall and filled many bags with beautiful dresses and modern outfits.

Once she was happy with all her new clothes, she stopped at the candy shop to purchase the Gummy Bears.

Lucy smiled at herself as she exited the mall, and practically skipped to her car in the deserted parking lot. She must have spent hours shopping, and she couldn't help but wonder if Cameron had missed her. She glanced around before dropping the shopping bags on the passenger seat, and then hopped over the door, into the car, and started the engine. The vibrations of the roaring machine set her soul on fire. It was only after she drove out of the parking lot that she noticed the van was following her again. The sun had retreated behind gray clouds, casting an eerie glow on the streets. The echoing sound of screeching tires reverberated through the narrow roads, sending Lucy's heart rate through the roof. It was too dark to make out the license plate, but fear made her step on the accelerator. The van followed her to the highway, where the landscape blurred into a whirlwind of lights and fuzzy forms.

Lucy clung to the wheel, adrenaline coursing through her veins. The van sped up leaving a small gap between itself and her car. She slowed and moved to the left, allowing it to pass, but it revved and swerved into her. Her car screeched as she straightened the wheels, trying to avoid it and sped up again. Her knuckles went white as she gripped the steering wheel, gasping for air. The anxiety in her stomach twisted into a tight knot, and with her jaw clenched, she hoped for a chance to survive this. As her car gained speed, the van pushed forward and caught up with her, closing in like a predator on the prowl. Lucy sped up more, but the van was fast enough to not leave her with any way out. She stepped as hard as she could on the pedal, but it was too late. Her body turned cold when she felt a force pulling her to the side, along with the disastrous bang vibrating through the air.

The van had swerved itself into the tail of Lucy's car, sending her car spinning off the road. Her stomach dropped as her vehicle became possessed, leaving her with no choice but to hold her breath and accept fate. As the tire hit the border stone, she bit hard on her teeth as it became airborne. The left side of the vehicle lifted off the ground, and she feared it would land on its side, or worse, roll. Luckily, she had put her seatbelt on, because just as the car lifted off the ground, it hit a streetlamp pole. The force of the crash sent her flying forward in her seat, and she heard her neck click as her head shot toward the windscreen. The airbag inflated with a pop, and she was forced back into her seat once again. The impact was sudden and jarring, leaving Lucy dazed and disoriented, the airbags enveloping her in a cloud of white. Panic flooded her senses as she struggled to regain her bearings.

As the wheels of the car finally stopped spinning in the air, everything came to a standstill, and Lucy could feel her weight pulling her down toward the right. Her first reaction was to massage her neck, and she hoped it had not been fractured. It had always been her very worst fear, being bound to a wheelchair. She wasn't sure what to do. While stuck to the seat, she was held only by her seatbelt. With her right shoulder leaning against the door, she tried to wiggle her legs free, but they were trapped between the seat and the steering wheel. While her mind flooded with flashing images repeating the situation, she could only piece together one sentence in her mind: "Dad would have killed me."

Some of the other cars pulled over and stopped. A worried voice called to her and asked if she was okay. Another voice shouted for someone to call an ambulance. Within minutes, the sound of sirens echoed through the tranquil countryside. Everything was a blur, and she couldn't make heads or tails of the voices.

"Keep still, love. Don't move." The paramedic was Lucy's calm in the turmoil.

Her passenger door was opened, and she heard someone yell, "Get her out before it blows!"

Lucy calmed her breathing and used her own common sense and stayed put.

"The car won't explode, don't listen to them." The soothing voice was close to her ear.

It took some time for the medic to free her legs and she was lifted from the car by many hands, her neck supported by something firm. Her body was moved, and she felt a cold, hard wooden board beneath her. She opened her eyes and saw the paramedic look down at her. It was an elderly lady with glasses.

"You're going to be fine, love. Just keep still and we'll do everything."

Her whole body shook, as she started shivering, feeling cold. As soon as she was safely strapped onto the stretcher, another medic draped a space-blanket over her. She knew from medical experience that hypothermia was one of the dangers after any trauma, so she welcomed the warmth.

Lucy looked up at the paramedic and in a desperate voice asked her, "Please get the Gummy Bears from my car."

"The other guys already collected your shopping bags, but I'll make sure we have them. Don't worry..." She disappeared for a moment and returned with the bag and showed them to Lucy. "These?"

"Yes."

The ambulance had its sirens on, and the vehicle drove fast. Every movement made Lucy want to gag, but she contained herself. All the way to the hospital, the medic, who had introduced herself as Thandi, spoke to her in her soothing voice, reassuring her that all was going to be okay.

She reached for Thandi's hand. "Someone deliberately forced me off the road," she managed to say.

"We'll inform the police for you, hun. As soon as we get you to the hospital. Just relax." She wrote something down on a clipboard, then turned her attention back to Lucy. "Are you in any pain, love?"

"No, I can handle it. It's not that bad."

"That's good news. Can you move your toes for me?"

Lucy moved her toes and Thandi looked satisfied.

The ambulance stopped and she knew they had reached the hospital. Thandi and the other medic pushed her into the ER. The bright lights burned her eye sockets. She blinked.

She heard the paramedics hand her over to the emergency room staff before she was transferred to another bed. She remained strapped in, for spine control, and they explained to her that she had to lie still like that until they had done x-rays of her spine.

Thandi leaned over her so that she could see her face. "Cameron called on your cell. She was worried that you weren't home yet. I told her what happened. She'll be here shortly."

"Thanks." Lucy started crying. Reality hit her with vengeance. Someone had tried to kill her. The car was most likely totaled.

The nurse was a middle-aged woman with dark hair. "Miss Donald, my name is Carla. You're in excellent hands, sweetie."

Lucy sniffed. "Okay."

Her caring smile was more than Lucy could bear, so she allowed her tears to flow freely.

The nurse continued comforting her without fail. "You're moving your toes and everything, so don't worry. This is all just routine."

Lucy knew that, but she didn't say she was also a nurse.

"Back again?" Dr. Johnson recognized her immediately. "Missed us, did you?"

"Couldn't resist the excellent care," Lucy said with heating cheeks.

After the doctor had examined her, he said, "We're sending you for x-rays."

It was like everything was happening at once. People rushing around, voices discussing her condition, hands touching her.

The nurse escorted Lucy to the radiology department, never once leaving her side. Lucy was grateful to her for her patience. The radiology unit was freezing, making her shiver even more. She knew it was just shock. *Click, click,* as the x-rays were done. Voices asking her questions. "Where is the pain? … Did you hit your head?"

Once they were finally done, Carla pushed her back to the emergency unit.

She heard Cameron's voice over the ER noise, asking frantically, "Where is she? Is she okay?"

"Your wife is in there, ma'am. Cubicle three."

A short moment later Cameron was at her side. Her face flushed.

"This seems familiar," Lucy mused when she saw her worried face. "Did they just call me your wife?"

"What happened?" She took hold of Lucy's hand and squeezed her fingers hard. "Are you hurting?"

"Only my fingers that you just broke."

Cameron sighed, her face looking anxious. "Sorry," she said and released her grip. "I should have gone with you. I shouldn't have let you go alone."

Another face appeared above Lucy. "Ma'am, I'm detective Sam Moore from the police department. The medic called me and told me you said someone deliberately pushed your car off the road."

"What? Who?" Cameron's voice sounded angry. "Could you see their face?"

"No, it was too dark." Lucy felt flustered. Cameron's anxiety was not helping.

"What type of car was it that did this to you? Lucy?" Cameron was in a state.

"Ma'am, you need to give her some room." The nurse touched Cameron's arm.

Cameron took a deep breath. Her voice was full of frustration. "Nobody's talking to me. I need to know what's going on." Lucy heard Cameron's voice drifting off as the nurse guided her away.

"Is now a good time to talk?" Sam asked.

"Yes," Lucy said. "I'm not hurt, I'm just in shock. A van forced me off the road. Oh no. I wrote off that beautiful car…"

Cameron was back again. "Lucy, we need to tell the police everything."

"It was a white van. That's all I know. Cameron, can you tell him about the other stuff? I'll listen and add if you leave anything out. I'm a bit fuzzy."

She listened as Cameron told the police everything, from the threatening letters to the possible poisoning. She didn't miss any of the details.

When Cameron was done giving Sam the statement, Lucy spoke. "Tonight, when I left my house, I saw the white van following me. I thought it was nothing at first, but when I left the mall, it was back. It was that same van that tried to kill me. They know where I live." Lucy sobbed. She could feel Cameron tensing beside her.

"We'll investigate, ma'am. I'll call you soon. Here," he reached into his breast pocket, "is my number. Call me if anything else comes up." He handed his card to Cameron.

"Good news, Lucy. You have no fractures. Probably just a sprain in your neck, some whiplash. You're all in one piece. How are you feeling?" The doctor flicked on a light and aimed it into Lucy's eyes.

She squinted. "I'm fine. The airbags saved my life." She whimpered. "I killed the car..."

"It was just a car, Lucy. I'm so glad you're okay," Cameron said, her voice sounding calmer. "Your mom has insurance on all the cars."

"I'm happy to send you home. If you experience any dizziness or vomiting, give me a call." He removed the neck collar the medics had put on her neck at the accident scene. "Hopefully you can stay away a little bit longer this time," he teased.

"I'll try."

Back in the car Cameron placed her hand on Lucy's knee and said in a stern voice, "You're not leaving my sight until we get to the bottom of this."

"Cameron, I hate feeling helpless. I can't be afraid the whole time. Maybe I should just go back home."

"I don't want to tell you what to do, but please know that whatever you decide, I'll support your decision."

"Hey, I got you your Gummy Bears," Lucy said before reaching into her pocket and pulling out the bag of candy.

Cameron laughed. "You lost a perfectly good Aston Martin Volante, but managed to save these?"

"You'd better share."

†

Frankie was seated at the dining room table when Cameron helped Lucy inside. "Dude, you look like you just crawled out of a hole. What happened to you?"

"She was in a car accident," Cameron said and pulled out a chair for Lucy.

"What? An accident? How?"

"I wrapped one of my dad's cars around a pole," Lucy said and looked at Cameron, begging with her eyes for her not to elaborate. "The pole was cold, and the Volante seemed like a perfectly warm blanket for it."

Cameron smiled and took the seat next to Lucy before pulling up a plate and packing it full of food for her. "No Gummy Bears for you until you finish all your vegetables, young lady," she said with a glint in her eyes. She proceeded to dish out a plate for herself.

"Don't be cheeky. I have them hostage right here in my pocket." Lucy picked at her plate for a while before taking a bite.

Frankie appeared uncomfortable watching them have an inside joke that didn't include her. "Babe, aren't you getting tired of running after this woman? There's always something with her, isn't there?"

"Not today, Frankie. Enough of your bickering. Lucy has been through enough."

"It's fine, Cameron." Lucy touched her arm before continuing, "Frankie, I understand that this is all very frustrating for you. Me being here, causing friction between you and Cameron and all, and I'm really sorry about that. It was never my intention."

"Yeah. I'm sorry too. I've been going through stuff..." Frankie's voice trailed off.

There was a long silence before Cameron pointed at her empty plate and announced, "Did you see? I chewed my food."

Lucy smirked. "At least one positive thing came from my time here." She placed the Gummy Bears in front of her. "You've earned these."

Her eyes lit up. "I will cherish them, thank you."

"Remember to be a good girl and share."

CHAPTER SEVEN

Two days had passed since the accident and since she saw Paul at the airport. Only two days, but it felt like many lifetimes. Cameron refused to let Lucy out of her sight during the day, and it took a lot of convincing on Lucy's part for Cameron to allow her to sleep alone in her room. Lucy took it easy, but except for the emotional trauma, she didn't have any physical after-effects from the accident. She was grateful for her miraculous survival and carried a newfound appreciation for life.

It was just after she had fallen asleep that she heard her door open. The draft on her face caused her heart to thump wildly against her chest. She opened her eyes and watched as the moonlight spilled through her bedroom window, creating a mystical glow in the room.

"*Lucy.*"

Lucy started. Goosebumps covered her skin and she squinted at the doorway, where the voice had come from. Had someone just whispered her name?

"*Lucy.*" The whispering sound of her name echoed off her walls.

Her body froze. She peered at her door, which was wide open, and the light of the moon reflected on a person standing there. She raised her torso up off the mattress, using her elbow as support as she tried focusing on the person standing there. She gasped. It was her mother.

Shocked, Lucy shot up. "Mom?"

Her mother turned and disappeared down the passage, toward the stairway. Lucy rolled out of bed and tiptoed to the passage, knowing that her mother did not have the power to walk all the way back down the stairs. But she had vanished into thin air. Her breath caught in her throat, and she couldn't breathe. She sprinted toward the staircase, and found it deserted. After flicking on the light switch, she darted down the stairs to Cameron's room. Without knocking, she rushed to Cameron's side where she was sound asleep. She touched her shoulder.

"Cameron," Lucy said in a panic.

She moaned and opened her eyes.

"It's my mom. Come."

Cameron wiped her face with the palm of her hand. She looked confused for a moment, not understanding.

"I think something's wrong."

Cameron hauled out of bed and followed Lucy down the flight of stairs to Angela's bedroom door. When they reached it, Lucy had completely lost her nerve. She stopped in the doorway, not ready for what she knew was awaiting them inside.

Cameron rushed past her, switched on the light and rushed to Angela's bed. She crouched down beside her and took her hand. "Angela, wake up."

She didn't move. She looked blue around the lips, her face lifeless.

Lucy stayed fixated to her spot. She felt like such a coward. In all her years of nursing nothing could have prepared her for this moment.

"Help, Lucy! I have no medical experience. What must I do?" Cameron's voice was high-pitched. She sounded desperate and her eyes were flooded with tears.

Hesitantly, Lucy crept closer to her mom's bed. It felt like an eternity until she finally reached her side, and when she felt her wrist for a pulse, there was none.

"Mom!" Lucy started shaking her, trying to wake her. "Mom! Please!" she exclaimed, hot tears flowing down her cheeks. "Come on, Mom! Not now! Not now, please," she cried, and when Lucy looked up at Cameron, she saw Cameron was sobbing. Lucy pressed the button on her bed to get her flat on her back and commenced with CPR. She wasn't in the Code Red emergency team for nothing.

Cameron stared at her with wide eyes when she started with cardiac compressions. "Stop, Lucy. This is not wat she wanted." She leaned over and touched Lucy's arm. "She's gone." Her voice was gentle. "I'm sorry…"

Lucy withdrew her hands from her mother's lifeless body, confused. Cameron was right. Her mother would kill her if she resuscitated her back to life.

"I saw her," Lucy said. "She called my name from my doorway. I saw her." Her legs gave way beneath her as she could feel her body go limp and before she sank down to the ground, Cameron caught her and supported her. Cameron wrapped her arms around Lucy and held her while they both cried.

Lucy had known this was going to happen, and yet it felt like her world had tumbled around her. She had hoped that there would still be time. There were so many unspoken words that she wanted to say. So much anger still locked inside that needed to be set free. All her opportunities were gone. This was the final moment. She would never get another chance.

"She came to say goodbye to you," Cameron whispered while holding her tightly. "She loved you."

"I know."

They stood there holding onto each other for a long while until a sudden intense calm enveloped her. An indescribable peace and strength from very deep within, and Lucy felt like she was being comforted by an invisible force. She sat on her mother's bed for a while, holding her icy cold hand, knowing she wouldn't get this moment with her again. Soon there would be arrangements to be made and people everywhere.

"Can I bring you some coffee? The sun is going to come up any minute now, we can go and watch the sunrise." Cameron's comforting hand rested on her lower back as she spoke.

"Sure, you go organize us some coffee and I'll call the doctor."

Cameron was her strength in that moment and Lucy knew she would always be grateful to her for that.

†

They took their coffees and walked over to the cliff, where they had taken Angela on so many occasions. Cameron sat on the rock and Lucy sat beside her.

As the dark, velvety blanket of night slowly receded, the world came alive with a gentle palette of colors. The horizon began to blush as the first rays of the sun ignited the sky, casting a warm golden glow over the tranquil ocean. Perched upon the rock, Lucy and Cameron sat in silent reverence, mesmerized by the beauty unfolding before them.

With each passing moment, the sky evolved, painting a breathtaking scene of nature's magnificence. The stars gradually faded into obscurity as the fiery sun ascended, creating a captivating display of hues. Deep blues melted into soft purples, which in turn transformed into delicate pinks and oranges. The kaleidoscope of colors danced across the water, a vibrant symphony of light and life.

Lucy closed her eyes, allowing the gentle sea breeze to caress her face, as if nature itself was whispering its secrets. The salty scent of the ocean mingled with the fresh aroma of morning dew, filling her senses.

As the sun continued its ascent, miniature diamonds scattered across the water, dazzling with an ethereal brilliance. The rhythmic undulation of the waves provided an enchanting backdrop, their soft melodies imbued with the promise of a new day.

Lucy marveled at the dance of the seabirds, as they gracefully skimmed the water's surface, celebrating the arrival of dawn. Their songs blended harmoniously, weaving a symphony with the gentle crash of waves against the shore. She wished she could join them, to feel the cool embrace of the ocean, and soar with the birds, free and weightless.

As the sun reached its zenith, the fiery glow transformed into a warm embrace, flooding the world with light and life.

Lucy reluctantly stood, taking one last long gaze at the masterpiece unraveling before her. The memories of this sunrise would forever be etched in her heart—the day her mother had passed and left this beautiful world. She would never witness this breathtaking view again, but she was finally free of the pain.

With a serene smile, she walked over to the edge of the cliff as she drank the last of her coffee. The colors were beautiful as the sun's rays warmed the horizon, and Lucy could feel her mother's presence as she stood there, watching. Cameron went to stand right beside her and put a comforting arm around her. She leaned her head on Cameron's shoulder and inhaled her scent.

"Are you okay?" Cameron asked after a long while.

"Strangely enough, I'm relieved. She went peacefully."

"Yes, I'm grateful for that, too."

"You're going to miss her," Lucy said.

"More than you could ever imagine."

"I should probably be heading back home as soon as the funeral is done." The thought of returning home made her heart ache, but she knew her time there was over.

Cameron's arm dropped and she straightened. "I wish you wouldn't go."

The words brought warmth to Lucy. "You know there's going to be a will, and we didn't exactly have a close relationship before she became ill. I'll have nowhere to go. She probably left everything to you." She didn't mean anything harsh with her words, as Cameron deserved to inherit the estate.

"Lucy," Cameron said and turned to face her. She took both her hands and continued, "Stay. Please."

†

A few days later, they had a small funeral. Everything flew by in a blur. Lucy wasn't sure what day of the week it was, and she wasn't sure what she was going to do next. Cameron and Lucy spoke, but only about the funeral arrangements. She was very supportive throughout the whole event, and it was as if everything just fell into place in no time. They had arranged to have her mother buried on the property. Cameron advised Lucy that it was what Angela had wanted. Only a few people came to the memorial, some had beautiful words of kindness to offer. It felt weird standing there, at the gravesite, when hardly anyone recognized Lucy. She felt out of place, standing there among mostly strangers. Some of them looked familiar to Lucy, but not all of them. She could see that Cameron tried to hold it together so she could be strong for Lucy, but Lucy knew Cameron was hurting too. She had lost a mother once before and this must've been so hard for her. Lucy's heart ached for Cameron, but for herself, too. All the years she had lost, she could have spent them with her mother. If only they had spoken. Lucy wished she had called her mother after her father had died ten years ago, but time travel wasn't possible, and she would live with the regret for the rest of her life.

Frankie was there too, of course, standing on the other side of Cameron. At least Frankie's services were no longer required there, and Lucy couldn't help but wonder what she was going to do after the burial. She would probably stay for the reading of the will, hoping to inherit something.

Her mind came back to reality when the speaker asked if anyone had any last words they wanted to say about Angela. Lucy swallowed and raised her hand. She stepped forward. Her heart raced, so she took a deep breath, raised her note that she had prepared, and started: "If someone had told me a few weeks ago that I'd be standing here right now, I would've told them they were crazy. I'm sure most of you believed the lies that I had died fifteen years ago, but as you can see, I'm right here."

There was loud muttering in the small crowd, but Lucy continued. "It's also no secret that my mom and I weren't on speaking terms these past fifteen years. But she still managed to bring me back here, with the help of someone I can now call a good friend." She looked at Cameron for a second and then continued. "These past few weeks have not been easy for me, but I'm glad I came to spend them with my mom. Even in her weakened state, she still managed to change me." Lucy looked down at the white casket hovering above the hole that would be her mom's final resting place. "I am a stronger woman now than ever before. In my mom's very last few days on this earth, she taught me about love and forgiveness." She looked up at Cameron, who smiled her reassurance. "Thank you," she said, stepped back to her side, and lowered the letter.

She felt Cameron's comforting arm around her shoulders and leaned into her warmth. A stray tear slithered down her nose to her lips and she wiped it away.

As the casket was lowered into the ground, the crowd started evaporating. Lucy sat down and watched as they covered it. By the time the hole had been filled, everyone had left except for Cameron. Cameron sat down beside her and reached for her hand.

"Your eulogy was beautiful," she said in a low tone.

Lucy stiffened for a moment before talking. "I'm ready to talk to you now," she said.

Cameron kept quiet and waited patiently for her to continue.

"My father used to visit my room at night after my mom had gone to sleep…" She choked back a tear before she continued. "It started when I was seven and never stopped until he got me pregnant at sixteen."

The shock in Cameron's face was evident. Lucy could hear Cameron swallow loudly. "Did your mother know about this?"

Lucy looked down at Cameron's hand holding hers. "I told her. Many times, but she didn't believe me. Or she was afraid, I don't know…" She shook her head.

"Oh my god…" Cameron's voice was filled with anger.

"My father denied it and when the pregnancy was confirmed, he told my mother that I was an attention-seeking whore. Then he sent me away. And she didn't stop him."

"That fucking asshole." That was the first time Lucy had ever heard Cameron swear.

"He paid a large sum of money into my bank account and told my mom that I was a slut and bad for the family's reputation."

"Lucy… I had no idea…" A tear rolled down Cameron's cheek.

"I pleaded with my mom, but she called me a liar and told me to leave quietly."

"Where did you go? You were just a child." Cameron gripped her hand tightly.

"I found a garden cottage in Ramsgate and took the bus." She hated the memories and wished she never had to relive the past again. "An elderly lady lived in the main house. Her name was Elizabeth. She was a nurse. If it wasn't for her… After a couple of months, I woke with terrible pains. There was blood everywhere. I didn't know what to do. I called my mom, but my father answered and told me she never wanted to speak to me again. Elizabeth took me to the hospital. I had lost the baby. It was such a relief, but I was so scared…"

Cameron shifted closer and placed her arm around Lucy. She pulled her very close and sounded out of breath when she spoke. "I don't know what to say…"

"Elizabeth's friends, the nursing staff at the hospital, were so amazing. It was there that I decided to become a nurse. Elizabeth helped me apply to nursing college and I was accepted. That's where I met Paul."

"Ah, we love Paul," Cameron said with a smile.

"You know, I always had anxiety when straight men tried to ask me out. With Paul I felt safe. I lived a mainly lesbian lifestyle, but never knew how to commit. Had the odd dates with men, but my hatred for men kept me from taking things further."

"I don't blame you. After what your father did to you. That sick fucking asshole!"

"One day, while working at the hospital, a patient was watching the news. My father had told the reporters during an interview that I had drowned. He was basking in the attention. Poor dad had lost his little girl."

"What a filthy piece of... If he was still alive, I would've killed him."

"I became promiscuous. With women. I think I needed to be validated and sex was the only way I knew how. Almost lost my job because of it."

"You felt safer being with women."

"Yes. I remember being drunk at parties and men groping at me, trying to get me to bed. It made me so angry. I hated them all."

"Oh, god, Lucy. I am so sorry…" Cameron sighed. "I wish I had met you sooner," she said, her voice filled with emotion.

†

It was hours since everyone had left after the funeral. There were lots of leftovers, as Connie seemed to have cooked the entire kitchen contents. The house felt empty. Lucy walked through her mother's room, and touched her things, feeling her presence in all her favorite belongings. She realized that it was only a matter of time before she had to return to Ramsgate. She would probably miss her childhood home. All the memories. She remembered how she and her mom used to go horseback riding almost every Sunday morning, and how her mother had sometimes dragged her along to her bridge club. She used to be so proud to show Lucy off to her friends. Her mom had loved lazing by the pool, sunbathing, and Lucy remembered the endless shopping they used to do together. Oh, how her mother loved to shop. She could spend hours at the high-end department stores.

This house held so many memories for Lucy, some good, some horribly bad. Her mom's hospital bed had been removed, and the king-size was back. Lucy picked up a teddy that was resting on the pillows. It used to belong to Lucy. She hugged it before replacing it. Lucy collapsed onto her mom's bed, pulled out her phone and called Paul. There were about ten missed calls from him. They had spoken, though, and he knew of her mom's passing.

He picked up on the first ring. "Hi, Sweetness, how are you keeping up?" Paul asked. "Missing you."

"Oh, my dear sweet Paulie. I miss you, too. So much."

"Wish I could be there for you. Couldn't find an available flight."

"I know. Sorry for not inviting you sooner."

"When are you coming home, Lucy? Alan and I would love to cook you a beautiful dinner and we can polish off his entire bar."

"Soon, I suppose. I must book my flight."

"You should wait until after the reading of the will, you know."

"There won't be a reading. Apparently, that only happens in the movies. Doubt she left me anything."

"Sweetie, I know you don't care about money and shit, but sometimes we need to stay put and listen to the universe."

"Paulie, even if my mother did leave me something, Cameron deserves to get it all. I just hope they sort this shit out soon. The staff need to know what's going to happen with their future. I'm sure they're worried."

"I can imagine. Going from a cushy job like that... . Promise me you'll wait until after the will has been delivered. I can come over, be there for you if you want. Alan will understand."

"I'll stay until next week. And no, Paul, no need for you to come over. You've always been there for me, and I truly appreciate that and love you to bits. But I'll be fine. I have Cameron here to stand by me through this."

"Ooh, Cameron?" His voice went a few octaves higher. "Do I sense some yearning in your voice when you say her name?"

"She is just a good friend. Like you. Nothing more," Lucy lied.

"Send her our love, too. She was very fond of your mom."

"I promise I will."

"I'll book your flight for you, okay? I'll book it for the end of next week, that way you'll be out of there in no time, and back with your favorite person in the world. Me. In the meanwhile, I'm here for you."

Lucy smiled. "Thanks, Paulie. You really are my favorite person in the world."

After she hung up, she lay on the bed and stared at the ceiling. It had been an exhausting day and she was tired. She knew the best thing to do was to pack her bags and return to Ramsgate. If she went home, she could be closer to her best friend, and her job. She needed to close this chapter and start a fresh one. In her heart, she really needed to get away. She soon drifted off to sleep, and when she awoke, the room was dark. She pulled out her phone and saw that it was almost morning. Wondering where Cameron was, she got up and went to her room. Cameron lay there in Lucy's bed, sound asleep. Lucy smiled. She must've fallen asleep while waiting for Lucy the previous evening. Lucy showered and prepared herself for the day that lay ahead. When she exited the bathroom, Cameron was still laying there, snoring softly.

After Lucy had made a pot of coffee, she poured a cup and went to sit at her favorite spot. The sea was rough, and the water sprayed as it hit the rocks down below. It was breathtakingly beautiful, even in the dark. She sipped her coffee and breathed it all in. Reality hit that she was once and for all an orphan. At thirty-one, she felt more lost and alone than ever. It scared her to death.

"There you are. I was looking all over for you."

Lucy jerked at the sudden interference into her thoughts. "God, Cameron, you startled me," she breathed.

"Gosh, I'm so sorry. Are you okay? You do realize it's five-thirty in the morning, don't you?"

"Yeah. I fell asleep on my mom's bed…" She swallowed. "Yes, I am fine."

"I brought some coffee, but I see you have one."

"Oh, mine is ice cold by now. Thanks." She chucked the last bit out of her mug and replaced it with the fresh cup Cameron had brought for her. Cameron sank down next to Lucy, on their rock.

193

"I waited in your room for you and then fell asleep. Hope you don't mind that I slept in your bed. It wasn't intentional."

"I have no problem with that, Cameron. Hope you slept well."

"I did, thanks. The lawyer called yesterday while you were in your mom's room. I didn't want to bother you. He's bringing copies of the will later today."

"That's good. Paul is booking me a flight for end of next week. I'll be staying for a while."

"Everything is so uncertain at this point. I only realized last night that I might have to head back to the UK. I don't know how that never crossed my mind before."

"Trust me, my mom would never do that to you. This will be your home forever." Lucy patted Cameron's leg gently. She could feel her muscles tense beneath her jeans.

"If she did that, then I want you to stay here. With me."

Lucy's heart raced. "Thanks for the offer, but I have a job, and strangely enough, I have friends too." She looked sideways at Cameron and winked.

"Lucy, I want you to understand something. I didn't take this job for the inheritance. I hated my job in England and was desperate for work and a family. It would mean a lot to me if your mother loved me enough to leave me a pot plant or a piece of furniture. But she would never have left me this house, or any of the other houses they owned for that

194

matter." Her serious tone changed into a playful one. "I would however love to inherit the yacht."

"I never knew they had a yacht."

Cameron sighed. "It's unimaginable. Have you been to any of their other villas?"

"Yes, I have. I have been to Mykonos, Hawaii, Italy, and Sweden. All their places are out of this world."

"I have been to some of those too. Your mother brought me along quite a few times. It was amazing."

Lucy shook her head in amazement. "Having a lot of money had always been my dad's main goal, which is probably why I don't let money rule my life."

Cameron became still next to her. "The sun's coming up."

The magnificent colors danced over the ocean, bringing forth a brand new day. Lucy inhaled the fresh air, wondering where life was taking her. In less than a month, she had become a completely different person.

They sat there until the sun was high above the horizon, talking about Cameron's experiences with Lucy's mother. After a while they went inside and had breakfast in the dining room.

It was almost lunchtime when Lucy was sitting by the pool, texting Paul, that the attorney arrived to deliver envelopes to the staff by hand. The butler, Robert, had let him in. Robert brought him to Lucy and introduced him.

195

"Ms. Lucy, this is the executor of your mother's estate. His name is Brett Fisher."

Lucy stood and took his outstretched hand. "Pleased to meet you, Mr. Fisher," she said. This was the part she had not looked forward to. Her time there would soon be coming to an end, and Lucy wasn't ready to let Cameron go. But she knew her old life was awaiting her, and soon she would have no choice but to return to Ramsgate. Even though Cameron had promised her she could stay, she had a sense that once Cameron inherited the house, she would change her mind and send Lucy packing. Money was evil that way. Lucy had first-hand experience.

"Please," he flashed his brilliant white teeth as he smiled, "call me Brett. My father is Mr. Fisher."

He spent a few minutes handing all the servants and gardeners each their own envelope. Lucy was relieved to see happy faces all around, which was proof enough that her mother had thought of her loyal staff. Most of them had been there for many years.

Cameron came to sit next to her, so Lucy put her phone down.

"Your mom was very generous. She apparently left each and every one a large sum of money. That way, if they lose their jobs here, they're sorted for a while before finding new employment."

"I'm happy she did." Lucy scanned their faces as they read their copies of the will, and suddenly wondered which one of them had been threatening her to leave, and why.

Claire walked up to where they sat. "I've come to thank you for everything you've done. That you brought peace and happiness to your mom before she passed," she said to Lucy.

"That's so sweet. Thanks, Claire," Lucy responded.

"My job was to look after her, and now that she's gone, I'm leaving. I just wanted to come and say goodbye." She came closer, leaned down and gave Lucy a quick hug. "I hope you make the right decisions for your future, Lucy." She then hugged Cameron and said, "It was good working side by side with you, Cameron."

"Do you have any plans?" Cameron asked.

"I have another job lined up for me. There's an elderly gentleman in need of care, and I've already accepted the position." She smiled sweetly before saying her last goodbyes and left.

Frankie sat by the bar, sipping on orange juice. Lucy watched as she received an envelope. Frankie looked thrilled as she pulled a document from it and started reading the one-page document. This was like Christmas with the executor being Santa. He finally turned to Cameron and Lucy and gave them each a thick envelope.

"Please go through these and let me know if you have any questions." He handed them each a business card.

"Thanks, Brett," Lucy said. Her stomach was in knots. She couldn't believe there was an envelope for her too, and she was curious what could possibly be inside.

"Wow, dude, your mom left me something too," Frankie said happily. "Two hundred thousand Rand, I can't fuckin' believe it."

"I'm happy for you, Frankie," Lucy said to her. She wasn't in the mood for her and hoped that Frankie would leave.

"Hell, I'm going shopping," she said. "Bye." And with that she was off.

Lucy looked down at the envelope in her hands. She pulled out a stack of papers. It was at least ten pages thick. Cameron's were too. She was glad for Cameron. That would mean that she didn't have to go back to England if she didn't want to. "Can I sit here and watch you read yours? I'm not ready to read mine yet. I'll read it later." Lucy stuffed her stash of papers back into the envelope.

Cameron scanned through the whole document quickly and looked up at Lucy with wide eyes. Lucy's stomach twisted in knots.

"What?" Lucy enquired softly.

"It's a lot…" She spoke quietly, in shock before she started reading it carefully.

Lucy watched her closely, the way her lips pursed as she read silently. Cameron smiled for a second, and then looked worried the next. She was sure she could see

Cameron's eyes go red at one stage. She frowned, blinked, and sighed out loud. She was taking longer than Lucy had expected, so she got up and went to the bar fridge. Connie always kept it stocked with beers, juice, waters, and ciders, and today was no different. She retrieved two bottles of cold water, and slammed the fridge shut with her foot. After opening both, she walked back to Cameron and gave her one.

"Thanks," Cameron said and took it. "You really should read yours," she said and looked at Lucy with confusion in her eyes.

Lucy did not like the sound of the strain in Cameron's voice. "What's it saying?"

"Read it," she insisted.

Lucy sat, opened her envelope again, and pulled the documents out. She started reading.

Lowering her copy after a long while, she looked up at Cameron. "I won't let you lose your inheritance. We'll call the lawyer, contest it, and once he signs everything over to you, I'll go back home," she promised.

"This document is legal and binding. Would it be so bad for you to stay here with me for a year?"

"A whole year? I'll lose my job, and I have friends at home."

"Your friends can come and visit you. Also, you'll never have to work again. Take a sabbatical."

"Cameron, you're asking me to leave my whole life behind," Lucy said to her, but deep down she had never felt more relieved. She wanted to stay with Cameron. She couldn't even begin to imagine life without her. This was the best gift her mother had ever given her. "I'm just going to make a phone call, then we can discuss this further."

"Take your time. I'm going to my room for a bit." Cameron seemed down.

Lucy got up and walked to the koi pond. She took her cell phone out and dialed Paul's speed dial.

"Yo, ho," he answered on the second ring.

"Compared to you and Alan, I am practically a virgin. You're the *ho*." She laughed.

"Stop beating around the bush, pun intended. What does the will say?"

"I'll scan it in and email it to you, but in a nutshell, I must stay in this house with Cameron for a full year. I'm not allowed to go back to Ramsgate, or else she won't inherit half the estate. And I am talking *estate*, as in all of the properties, including the ones in Europe, Hawaii, Paris, heck I can't even remember the rest. Paul, I'm talking about eight luxurious properties. A yacht that is worth millions. If I leave at any time, Cameron won't inherit a thing."

She heard Paul gasp as she broke the news to him. "And what about you? Do you get anything?"

"If I stay, I get fifty percent and Cameron gets the other half. If either one of us leaves, none of us gets anything, then everything will be donated to my dad's sucky water-selling company. Can you imagine? Quite frankly, I don't give a shit about any inheritance, but if I don't stay, Cameron gets nothing. She might then have to go back to the UK."

"How does Cameron feel about all this?"

"She wants me to stay..." Lucy sighed into the phone and swallowed back a lump.

"Looce, that's so awesome... I'm happy for you, girl."

"What should I do, Paulie?"

"Sweetie... I'll visit you, okay?" His voice broke and she wished he was closer so she could hug him. "What do I do with your flight ticket that I booked for next week, want me to cancel it?"

"No, I have to come get my stuff and find a tenant for my house. Oh yes," she gulped, "I have to resign my job."

"First of all, I will help you find a tenant for your house. Secondly, don't you have to work a calendar month when you resign?"

"Not if I give them immediate notice," Lucy said. "My resignation month will be the rest of my leave days."

"I'll fetch you from the airport. Can't wait to see you."

"You're my best friend, Paul. I love you," Lucy said, feeling sad that he lived so far.

"Love you too, peanut." He made kissing sounds into the phone, which she returned before they said goodbye.

After ending her call with Paul, she went up to Cameron's room. She knocked, and when there was no answer, Lucy opened the door and entered. Cameron sat on her bed, staring at the documents that were spread out in front of her. She looked up at Lucy for a second, and then back down at the papers again.

"How many times have you read through them by now?" Lucy mused.

"Hundred, three hundred times, I don't know." She sighed. "I just can't get to the bottom of this. Why would your mom do this?"

"Beats me," she said. "I'm sure she had her reasons."

"I guess I wasn't really preparing myself to return to the UK so soon. This has been my home for five years. I suppose I could apply for another job and stay in the country, but with the unemployment rate being so high, it's like finding a needle in a haystack."

"You don't have to go." Lucy walked over to Cameron and sank down beside her. Cameron looked at her with hope in her eyes. "I'll stay," Lucy said softly.

"No, you can't do that for me—"

"I want to stay."

The relief on Cameron's face was evident. "Really? You'll stay?"

"I'm not going anywhere," Lucy reassured her. "As long as you can tolerate a lot of Paul. He's going to be here more than you can handle. I'm buying him plane tickets for every month for the next year."

Cameron laughed. "It's going to be a hoot." Her eyes went tender. "Lucy, it's not the money, the estate, or the yacht that I want. It's you… I wasn't ready to lose you."

"Well, now you don't have to."

CHAPTER EIGHT

Boarding the flight after spending all that time in Cape Town felt like it had been years and at the same time merely hours since Lucy had left Ramsgate. She wondered how it would feel walking into her house again and being there all alone. A few weeks ago, she would have thought nothing of it, but now all she could think of was Cameron and getting back to her as soon as possible. She tried to clear her mind, but the harder she struggled, the more thoughts of Cameron clouded her brain. The two-hour flight was over in a minute, and walking through the domestic arrivals terminal made her feel like there was a spotlight on her, and the whole world was watching her. Lucy had barely gone three steps through the gates when she was attacked by a huge teddy bear. Paul was on top of her, and she couldn't breathe, the way he held her so hard. He still hadn't shaved.

"Oh, Lucy. I missed you so much," he squealed. She hugged him as tight as her arms would allow, and he finally let go of her so she could have a good look at him.

Lucy regarded him with a mix of curiosity and wonder. "Looks like your man wanted to keep his cuddly bear for a bit longer." She patted his face. "Looking great." She laughed at his massive grin.

"I see Cape Town was not so good for you. Look at the state of your hair, so neglected. And you've lost weight. And why are you wearing blue and orange in the same outfit? Your clothes don't even match your luggage."

Lucy looked down at her chosen attire, and she didn't think the colors looked that bad, but then again, she had no fashion sense.

"Can you stop already? I'm here now, and that's all that matters."

"Na-uh. I have a week off, which is time for me to spend with you, and only you." He flapped with his hand as if squatting at a fly. "We're going on a spending spree. You're having a makeover. I am taking you to my hairdresser. Look how divine my hair is." He spun around in a circle, ballerina-style, showing off his neatly cropped hair, with his new highlights. "And you're having those bushy eyebrows waxed."

"I will have my face waxed if you do yours, too." She grinned.

"And lose my sexy charm? Not on your life." He declined any say Lucy thought she could possibly have.

"Well, I guess I'm in your hands then, buddy."

"Let's get you home first." He took Lucy's bag from her. "This is so light. Did you bring anything?"

"I only brought a few bare necessities. I was thinking of packing all my clothes into boxes and dropping them at Goodwill."

"Oh, those poor people," he joked. "Now they must suffer too."

Lucy laughed and rolled her eyes. "I also want to donate all of my money that my dad gave me when I was sixteen to the hospital I'm resigning from. It has increased a lot since I invested it."

"Seriously?" Paul paused while he dumped her bag in his trunk.

"They've been good to me," Lucy explained before clambering into Paul's car. He had a nifty little sports car that Alan had given him for one of their anniversaries.

"You're right. They kept you on the payroll even after you *hanky panky'd* with the patients—"

"And some of the staff," Lucy interjected. "Did you print my resignation letter that I emailed you last night?"

He pointed at the glove compartment. "It's in there."

She took the letter out, found a pen in the tiny space and signed the bottom just in time before Paul pulled out of the parking spot.

†

Lucy knocked on the door.

"Enter," said a voice muffled from inside.

She walked into the clinical room and saw Matron Sally Smith's face light up when she saw her.

"Hi," Lucy said.

"Well, well, well. Look what the cat dragged in. How's your mother?"

"She passed almost two weeks ago."

"I'm so sorry, Lucy. Sit down. Can I organize you some tea?"

"Actually, I've come to give you this." Lucy put the piece of paper on her desk and slid it toward her.

Sally reached for it, picked it up, and read the letter of resignation. "Immediate notice. You sure?"

"Yes, Sally. I have some business to attend to and I'm going to need a year at least."

"Lucy, hospital policy states that once you give such a short notice you can never come back. We can never employ you again."

"I'm aware of that, but I don't have a choice," Lucy said.

The corners of her lips raised a little. "I'm going to miss sneaking around with you."

Lucy smiled. "I'm sure you'll find someone else to keep you occupied. Also," Lucy slid the cheque across her desk, "I want to donate some money toward the ER department. Perhaps the hospital can use it to treat victims of sexual abuse that can't afford it."

Sally gasped when she looked at the amount on the cheque. "That is very kind of you, Lucy. Thank you." She got up, reached her hand across the desk and Lucy shook it. "Best of luck for your future. Look me up if you're ever in the area again."

"Thank you."

†

After the visit to the hospital, Paul bought them some Chinese takeout and then dropped Lucy off at home. He took her bag from his trunk, handed it to her and said, "I promise I'll be here early tomorrow morning and I'll bring empty boxes."

"Thanks for the ride. Kiss Alan for me."

"On the lips?"

"Yes." Lucy grinned.

He laughed, waved, and drove off.

Lucy entered her house, dropped her bag in her room, and then walked around slowly. It felt empty and lifeless.

She wondered how she had survived there all these years. She took her food, sat on the couch, and flipped on the television. She stared at the screen while eating her food, not concentrating for a moment. She couldn't think of anything else but Cameron. Even though she had only been a part of Lucy's life for about a month, she occupied her every thought. How could someone have such a major effect on a person? Cameron had entered her life, ruffled it up, and messed with her head. Not intentionally, that part Lucy knew. She had been comforting and made Lucy feel safe and protected. She had seen Cameron that morning, yet she missed her. How was it possible to miss her already?

Lucy looked down and noticed that her food was finished, so she walked to the kitchen and threw away the empty containers. She had to find something else to occupy her mind. Missing Cameron was driving her insane. She suddenly remembered Paul's offer to do a makeover, and she really wanted to look good for Cameron when she returned. She wanted Cameron not to be able to keep her hands off her. She wanted her to yearn for her as much, she realized, as she was for Cameron.

At that moment, her phone buzzed. She raised it and looked at the screen. *Cameron*. Lucy took a long, slow breath before answering.

"How's Ramsgate?" Cameron's voice was low. Lucy welcomed it. She wanted to hear it all day and night.

"It's dead quiet here, and I must admit, I'm feeling quite lonely. What are you up to?"

"We just had dinner, and we decided to watch a movie."

We? Her heart sank down to her shoes. She wondered if her next year would be spent with Frankie too. "Is Frankie planning on staying there?" Lucy wished she could take back the question, as she was afraid of the answer. How was she going to survive living with Frankie for a year? Especially seeing as Lucy was dying to be alone with Cameron.

Cameron was quiet for a while. "Uh. I'm not sure. It's something we definitely need to discuss."

"What movie are you guys going to watch?" Lucy's stomach did a nervous twist as she awaited the response, hoping it wasn't something romantic. She could imagine Frankie all over Cameron in her short dress, trying to seduce her.

"Some or other horror, not sure."

That was even worse. Lucy cringed. She wasn't usually the jealous type.

"Are you still there?" Cameron's low, gentle voice brought her back to reality.

"Sorry, I was just sidetracked for a second."

"You must be under a lot of stress right now. Take it easy," she said. "And hurry on back home. I miss you."

"I miss you, too, Cameron," she said softly.

"Sleep tight."

"You too." Lucy reluctantly ended the call. She missed her even more now. What was Frankie up to? Horror movie? Lucy shuddered. She shouldn't have left. What if Frankie finally managed to seduce Cameron? Why did that even matter to her, Lucy wondered.

That night, as she lay in bed unable to sleep, it dawned on her. She was falling in love. The realization hit her like a gentle breeze, slowly stirring the depths of her emotions. At first, she had been captivated by Cameron's undeniable beauty, drawn to her physical allure. But now, as she replayed their conversations in her mind, reminisced about their shared moments, and contemplated the bond they had forged, she recognized a deeper connection.

It wasn't just about appearances anymore, it was about the way Cameron made her feel. Her laughter echoed through her thoughts, their conversations resonated in her heart, and their shared experiences had etched themselves into her memories. She found solace in Cameron's presence and comfort in her words.

With every passing day, her admiration for Cameron had transformed into something more profound. Much more meaningful than mere attraction. She began to understand the essence of love—the intangible force that binds souls together. Love, Lucy realized, was not solely based on physical appearance, although it could certainly be the initial spark. It ran deeper than that, permeating every aspect of their connection. It was the way Cameron's imperfections only made Lucy love her more.

As she lay in bed, thoughts swirling, she couldn't deny the truth any longer. Love had found its way into her heart, whispering soft melodies of affection and infatuation. The journey had started with attraction, but it had grown into something far more profound—an undeniable love for Cameron. And as sleep finally embraced her that night, she knew that she was heading down a path filled with both excitement and uncertainty, ready to embrace the beauty and complexity of loving another human being.

†

By the time Paul arrived the following morning, she had packed everything on her bed and they just needed to be packed into the boxes he had brought. It took them an hour to pack, after which they dropped the boxes off at Goodwill. He then drove Lucy to the hairdresser and chose a hairstyle for her, because according to him, she had *zero* taste.

The hairdresser colored Lucy's hair golden blond and blended some bronze strips in. After that, he layered it and made it feathery, using a blade. Lucy had to admit, the new hairstyle made her eyes look bigger, and she felt younger. Sexy.

Once they were done at the hairdresser, Paul led her to the beauty parlor, where her eyebrows were done and then her nails. Lucy opted for a clear varnish and declined the acrylics.

Paul clapped his hands eagerly at the result. "Girlfriend, you are going to turn heads!" he exclaimed. "Now, we're going clothes shopping, and like your hairstyle, I'm picking your outfits."

The possibilities seemed endless as they centered their attention on a quaint boutique that caught their eye. Its vibrant sign beckoned them inside, promising a treasure trove of fashionable finds.

The moment they stepped into the store, their senses were overwhelmed by the array of colors, textures, and styles. They couldn't contain their eagerness and began browsing different racks filled with unique clothing items, each whispering stories of its own.

"How will this dress look on me?" Paul held up a colorful, tight little number in front of him.

"Never knew you were into cross-dressing, but that will look ravishing on you," Lucy said.

He squealed. "I'm buying this. Wonder what Alan's going to say."

Lucy picked out a whimsical floral sundress that seemed to call her name. Meanwhile, Paul found the perfect pair of statement earrings that shimmered under the store's warm lighting. He held them up to Lucy's face and nodded his approval.

After trying on their newfound treasures, they modeled in front of the mirror, giggling with delight. They decided to check out and continue their shopping spree through other stores, exploring the bustling shops at the mall.

Once they had filled bountiful bags with clothes, Paul suggested they visit a local market nearby that was known for its delectable treats. As they wandered through the market, the aromas of fresh fruits, baked goods, and exotic spices enveloped them. The colorful display of produce enticed them, and they indulged in samples of juicy strawberries, artisanal cheeses, and mouthwatering pastries.

With their bags filled with new clothing, shiny accessories, and delicious treats, they made their way back to the car, their hearts dancing with joy and their eyes beaming with satisfaction. As they rode to Paul and Alan's home, they reflected on the memorable day they had had, cherishing the bond they shared as friends.

After brainstorming the perfect menu, Paul prepared dinner. First on the menu was a vibrant salad with crisp greens, juicy tomatoes, and a tangy balsamic vinaigrette. It was a refreshing and light choice to start their meal.

For the main course, he prepared what he called his signature dish, creamy mushroom risotto. He knew Lucy had always been a fan of this rich and flavorful dish. Finally, for dessert, Paul decided to surprise Alan and Lucy with a homemade apple pie. The sweet aroma of cinnamon and freshly baked apples wafted through his kitchen as the pie crust turned golden and flaky in the oven. Paul knew that nothing would bring a smile to Lucy's face quite like a slice of warm apple pie, with a very large dollop of whisked cream.

Alan was pleasantly surprised to see Lucy again and after they had enjoyed their culinary delights, Paul showed him the new dress he had bought.

"Mm. When Lucy leaves, you are going to dance for me, my angel," Alan purred with excitement written all over his face.

"I guess that's my cue to leave," Lucy said.

After they said their goodbyes, Paul dropped her off at home.

†

They spent the rest of their week together, eating a lot, and shopping even more. Cameron called her daily to check in, and Lucy accepted each call with fervor.

The atmosphere was somber on their last evening together. Paul and Alan took Lucy out to dinner at one of their favorite restaurants. She was sure she had gained back all the weight that she had lost in Cape Town, but she had never felt healthier.

All night long, Alan couldn't keep his hands off Paul. It was so nice seeing them so happy.

Lucy was sad, because she would miss Paul tremendously. She knew they would visit often, but it would be difficult not having her best friend just down the road. The sadness she felt for leaving Paul behind was overridden by her excitement to see Cameron again. Lucy had never known it was possible to miss another human being that much.

The following morning, the atmosphere was somber as Paul took her to the airport. Lucy gave him her house and car keys, as he had promised to sublet it and donate the money to the hospital. They could keep her car as a spare or donate it if they wanted to. He was quiet most of the way, and Lucy didn't know what to say in order to make the pain less.

He helped with her bags that were much heavier than when she'd arrived, and by the time they reached the boarding gates, a river of tears was flowing from both their eyes.

"Paul, promise you'll visit?"

"Every month. But that doesn't make it easier. I'm going to miss you." His voice was higher than usual as he tried to speak through the tears.

Lucy draped her arms around him and hugged him as hard as she could. "Same here. Call me whenever you can."

It's never easy saying goodbye to a friend, and by the time Lucy pried herself away from Paul's arms, she realized that she had almost missed her flight. Paul was one of those dramatic types, one of those special people that would run through the airport, trying to follow the plane. Paul was one of those. When Lucy looked from her tiny little window on the plane, she could see him running, wrists in the air, bag flung over his shoulder, scarf blowing back from the force of the speed, through the viewing area.

Lucy laughed after she swallowed down the tears as she watched him. She knew he was putting up a show just for her amusement.

†

Cameron had spotted Lucy before she noticed her. She stood tall and proud, holding the iPad with Lucy's name, exactly like that first day they met. She looked even more beautiful than she had back then. Lucy's heart skipped many beats when their eyes met, and Cameron smiled at her. She lifted Lucy off the ground once her arms were around Lucy, their bodies fit perfectly.

"God, I missed you," Cameron said loud enough for everyone around them to hear.

"I missed you, too."

Her face beamed when she took the luggage trolley from Lucy and led the way to the car.

"Thank goodness no limo today," Lucy said when she spotted the Jeep.

"Didn't want to embarrass you like that again." Cameron laughed. "By the way, Olaf decided to retire in three months, so there will be no driver soon." She ruffled Lucy's hair. "I absolutely love the new hairdo."

"Paul's idea," Lucy confirmed. "He took me for a makeover."

"You always look beautiful," Cameron said, glancing at her sideways. "Ready to get home?" She opened the car door and helped Lucy in. Afterward she placed Lucy's luggage in the back and hopped into the driver's side.

"Ready as I'll ever be."

"I have something for you," she said and held out her hand.

"One Gummy Bear?" Lucy exclaimed.

"Told you I'd share."

CHAPTER NINE

"What's for dinner?" Cameron came to join Lucy in the kitchen.

Lucy had given Connie the rest of the evening off, so that she could cook. Connie had decided to stay, which was a relief, as Lucy had grown to truly like Connie.

Cameron came to stand behind her and peeked over her shoulder at the pots on the stove. She was so close, Lucy could feel her breath on her neck, and if Lucy turned her head ever so slightly to the right, their lips would be only inches apart. She inhaled and closed her eyes.

"What *is* that?" Cameron asked again, referring to the pot bubbling on the stove top. Her voice was low, and her lips were close to Lucy's right ear.

Lucy felt her hands move and she placed them on Lucy's sides, resting them on either side of her waist. She leaned back a little until Cameron's body was plush with hers. It felt like they were melting into one another. She had missed the way Cameron held her. Her hands moved up slowly until they reached just below her breasts and down again to the sides of her hips. Cameron's warm breath caressed the skin on the side of her throat softly. Her hands gripped with more pressure as she pulled her hips into her. Warmth radiated off Cameron's body and seemed to penetrate Lucy's soul. Cameron lowered her head until her face touched Lucy's neck and breathed her in deeply. Lucy felt dizzy with need for her. Why wouldn't she kiss her already? Or was she waiting for Lucy to make the first move?

Lucy turned slowly, Cameron's arms still at her waist. Once she faced Cameron, she opened her eyes. Cameron looked down at her. Lucy slid her fingers up Cameron's arms and held onto her shoulders. Her knees went weak. Her chest heaving as she tried catching her breath. Cameron leaned closer, their faces almost touching. With her hands grasping the material of Lucy's dress at the back, she pulled Lucy's hips flush with hers and kissed Lucy. Her lips were soft and hard at the same time. She opened her mouth and hungrily sucked Lucy's lips, biting softly and groaned. Lucy slipped her arms around Cameron's neck and pulled her closer. Cameron devoured her mouth, while her hands pressed hard against her lower back. Lucy could feel Cameron's hips move, her breathing increasing, and her hands gripping at her back.

Cameron kissed her for a long time before she finally pulled back. "Been wanting to do that for a very long time," she said, out of breath. Then added, "There's smoke behind you."

Lucy jumped back around. Her cheeks flushed. She quickly picked up a spoon and stirred the stew. "You burned the food," she said.

"I'm sorry," she said. "Pizza?"

Lucy laughed. "I'll get the wine."

†

Cameron went to the door and paid the delivery guy for the pizzas while Lucy set three places at the dinner table. She had chosen a bottle of 2006 Côte-Rôtie Shiraz, and seeing as she didn't know much about wine, she secretly hoped it was a good year. While Lucy opened the bottle and poured them each a glass, Frankie helped Cameron carry the food to the table.

"So, Frankie. Got any future plans?" Lucy hoped she didn't sound too blunt, but she needed to know.

Frankie's eyes went wide as she glared at Lucy. "I see I've overstayed my welcome." The sound of disgust was evident in her voice. She reached for a slice of pizza.

Cameron placed two slices on her plate before taking a sip of wine. She examined Frankie's face for a minute before she spoke. "Frankie, I truly appreciate everything you did for Angela and if you ever need anything, you are more than welcome to call. But I agree with Lucy. We can help you find a place."

"But I only got two-hundred thousand Rand. I can't do anything with that," she insisted, pouting her lips.

"That's more than enough for a deposit and a whole year upfront on a very nice place," Cameron explained. "You still have your job at the hospital pharmacy."

Frankie pushed her chair away from the table and faced Lucy. "This is all your fault! Everything was going according to plan until you came along. I wish you had died in that car crash." She stormed off, taking her plate with her.

Cameron looked stunned. She shot up and went after her. Lucy remained at the table, surprised at Frankie's sudden outburst. She helped herself to a slice of pizza.

A little while later, Cameron returned. "I can't believe she said that. I asked her if she had anything to do with your accident, and she denied it. But her behavior is totally uncalled for."

"I want her out. Now more than ever," Lucy said softly. "I don't trust her."

"I'll make sure she's out before the end of the week."

†

After dinner, Cameron and Lucy cleaned the kitchen together. Lucy had to chuck all the stew she had made, as it was completely ruined. Cameron made some hot chocolate and once they were done, Cameron said, "I don't think it's a good idea for you to sleep alone tonight. Would you like to sleep in my room?"

Lucy nodded in agreement and followed Cameron to her bedroom. Once inside, Cameron took her cup from her and placed it on the side table. She then turned to face her. Lucy felt nervous. This was the first time she had ever felt this way about anyone, and she was afraid of messing things up. Cameron placed her arms around Lucy and kissed her deeply. Lucy slid her hands around Cameron's neck, welcoming her lips. Cameron felt so good. As her fingers travelled to the inside of Cameron's collar, she gently stroked the skin in her neck and a groan escaped Cameron's throat. Her kiss deepened and her arms tightened around Lucy. She could feel Cameron's passionate response, which excited Lucy even more. She wanted to give her all to Cameron but hesitated for a split second.

Cameron pulled away. "You can relax. Nothing needs to happen tonight."

"But I want you," Lucy responded in a husky voice.

"Things are moving a bit too fast for me. Do you mind if we slow things down a bit?"

"Absolutely."

"Lay down," Cameron instructed.

Lucy obeyed. Cameron followed suit and they lay for a moment facing each other. Lucy's heart raced, and time seemed to stand still as Cameron delicately brushed a strand of hair behind her ear. With a captivating mix of nervousness and excitement, Lucy leaned in, and their lips finally met again, in a tender embrace. It was as if the world melted away, leaving only their connection and the electrifying touch of their lips. Cameron kissed her, gently at first, but her kisses deepened with every breath. Her hands were on Lucy's lower back. Her palms pressing Lucy into her. With quickening breath, Lucy kissed her back. She was hungry for more of her. Cameron's body was pressed hard against her and it felt good.

They kissed for a long time, until Cameron finally pulled away. She was practically panting. "I think we need to stop before we get too carried away," she said.

"Of course," Lucy agreed.

Cameron sat up and passed Lucy her hot chocolate that had started cooling.

Lucy took a sip and cleared her throat. "Have you ever been in love?"

"Yes. It was one of the reasons I left the UK. Besides hating my job, that is. My girlfriend of six years cheated on me with my best friend. Sounds cliché, I know."

"So you left the whole country?"

Cameron grinned. "Anna cheating on me wasn't the only reason I left the country. The other parts I already told you were true."

"I'm so sorry that happened to you…"

"I'm not. My life took a 180 degree turn for the better. Your mom was more of a mother to me than mine was. Then I met you." Cameron looked at Lucy, her eyes tender.

"Wait… Have you been celibate during your entire stay in South Africa before you met me?"

"I have."

"Still getting over Anna?"

Cameron laughed. "I have been over Anna for a long time. I just never had time."

"You have all the time in the world now."

"How about you, Lucy? Past relationships?"

"Many, but never been serious about anyone. I was seeing a therapist for a while, who assured me it was absolutely normal after the abuse I suffered from my father. I guess I never trusted anyone until now."

Cameron leaned closer to her and said, "I hope you will learn to trust me. I will never hurt you."

They sat until late, discussing the will and the yacht. Cameron's face lit up every time the yacht was mentioned, and she promised to take Lucy for a picnic on it as soon as Frankie had moved out and settled into her new place. Cameron finally pulled the blanket over them and held onto Lucy until they both eventually drifted off to sleep.

225

CHAPTER TEN

A week later, Lucy gaped as they stood in front of *Sea Biscuit*, which was an enormous engine-driven yacht, floating lazily on the water at the docks. Cameron boarded the vessel first, then proceeded in helping Lucy with the food basket and their backpacks. Lucy had never seen such a magnificent structure in all her life.

"Can I take you on the grand tour?" Cameron offered with a proud smile.

Lucy nodded happily and followed her lead.

The *Sea Biscuit's* unique layout provided accommodation for up to ten people. The interior was finished in high gloss African cherry wood. Lucy ran her fingers over the surface that felt smooth and silky. She realized her mouth was hanging wide open in shock as she followed Cameron who seemed so at home there, dressed in jeans, a spaghetti top, and a cowboy hat. Cameron led her to a country-style kitchen, or as Cameron called it, the galley, with granite counter tops, stove, microwave, and dishwasher. A dinette with seating for up to ten faced the galley. Directly across from the galley was a stairway leading up to the sky-lounge and helm station. On the deck, Lucy was fascinated that the yacht was equipped with a jacuzzi and multiple loungers.

When they reached the helm station, Lucy noticed Olaf at the steering wheel, awaiting their thumbs-up before starting up her engine. Up until that moment, Lucy had been wondering if Cameron had planned on sailing the boat on her own and, Lucy had to admit, she was secretly relieved to see that they had someone with a skipper's license.

"Glad to see you're not planning on driving this thing," Lucy teased Cameron.

"Me? Oh hell no. But I'm planning on getting my license one of these days. God, I love this thing."

"I was afraid you would crash *Sea Biscuit* and then we would have to change her name to *Limp Biscuit*."

"Funny," she said and faked a laugh. "You have no faith in me, do you?"

The weather was perfect, with only a slight breeze to cool off the sun's hot rays. After removing her jeans and shirt, Cameron sat on a lounger, wearing nothing but a bikini

227

and her hat. Lucy removed her dress and joined her, occupying the lounger right next to hers. It felt great spending the whole day with Cameron, not having to worry about anyone else. *Especially Frankie.*

"Glass of wine for you?" Cameron opened one eye and peered at her from beneath her tilted cowboy hat.

"In the sun?" Lucy adjusted her bikini top. "I'll have a water, thanks."

"Ay, Cap'n," Cameron said. She raised her gorgeous body from her lounger, and Lucy could admire her form for a moment without Cameron noticing. When Cameron leaned down to retrieve two waters from the cooler, Lucy watched the muscles dance in her back. Lucy bit her lower lip. When Cameron turned from the cooler, she raised an eyebrow at Lucy. "Like what you see?" She grinned.

"You're so full of it." She flung her dress at Cameron, which Cameron caught, almost dropping the bottles of water.

Cameron handed her a bottle of water and sat back down again. "Things are so peaceful now that Frankie's gone," she said.

"I'm so glad we found her a beautiful place. No excuses for her to stay anymore. I can finally relax. I never trusted her."

"Pity things turned out the way they did for her. Guess she brought it all on herself, though."

"Cameron," Lucy said and paused, "I know you said you never had time for relationships, but I have to know, did you and Frankie ever have a thing? Or a fling?"

"She wanted us to, but like I've said before, I wasn't attracted to her."

"That night you guys went to the movies and watched that horror film?"

"We didn't go to the movie theatre, we watched at home."

"Even worse…"

"She tried, but I pushed her away. Told her that I was interested in you." Cameron offered a skewed smile and winked.

"Really?"

"You don't think there's a spark between us?" She frowned.

Lucy reached over and touched Cameron's arm with her fingertips, and for a moment she could feel Cameron tremble. Cameron's eyes locked onto hers and the energy field that enveloped them increased in strength. For a moment Lucy had forgotten to breathe, leaving her dizzy. Her mind had frozen in space and time and would not, *could not*, continue to function as normal. During her moment of not breathing, she had noticed Cameron's breathing had gained pace. Thoughts of them, skin on skin, tongues in duel, fingers stroking, had Lucy in turmoil. Neither of them spoke for a while, as they stole glances from each other in silence.

Lucy broke their intimate contact for a moment and looked on the deck where there was a hammock, perched to one side. It was in full shade. Not wanting to burn in the sun, she got up and moved toward it. It looked comfortable, so she dropped her body into it.

Cameron walked over to her.

"May I join you?" she asked seductively.

"Be my guest." Her heart rate had accelerated again, and her body was on fire with the thought of Cameron's body so close to hers. Especially with them both being in nothing but their bikinis. Cameron removed her hat, carefully climbed on and snuggled right up against her. The heat from Cameron's skin penetrated her, and her magnetic field reeled Lucy in, like an invisible force. Lucy found it hard to control herself. Leaning on an elbow, she looked down at Cameron. Cameron's eyes were hot and waiting. Lucy could see her pulse thumping in her neck.

"Kiss me alread—" Cameron whispered.

The last word was not even uttered in full yet when her lips met Cameron's mouth. Her longing for Cameron was excruciating. They were instantly one, sucked in by a fervor Lucy had ever only experienced with her. Cameron's tongue darted from between her lips, teasing. Cameron's hand found the warmth of Lucy's lower back, and started caressing her skin softly at first, but it then proceeded in gripping her to pull her closer into her. As one, they were floating on the sea of love and lust, drifting off to a place where no man had ever been before. Their bodies were like two magnets stuck together. Lucy felt Cameron's hand moving up to the front of her body and caressing her breast softly, fingers taking in every detail of her glorious erect nipple. Her arms wrapped around Cameron, holding onto her, beckoning her for more.

Cameron moaned softly, her lips never once leaving hers. Lucy's sensitive skin took in every perfect detail. Cameron's body was a part of hers. And vice versa. Nothing else existed but them, in their cocoon of desire. They kissed each other for a long time, exploring, feeling the need for more growing intensely, but neither of them crossed that line. Lucy's hips moved against Cameron's. She could feel Cameron's body shiver, as Cameron was grinding hard against her groin. Pulling her mouth away from Cameron's was excruciating, and the longer they kissed, the harder it was to stop. Lucy sighed when Cameron finally pulled her head away and looked up at her. The hunger in Cameron's eyes made her ache even more. Cameron's fingers were entwined with her hair at the back of her neck. She had left her wanting. Begging. For more.

She bent down and kissed and nibbled Cameron's neck. Cameron's fingers dug into the skin on Lucy's back. "Fuck. Don't do that," she groaned as her lips found Lucy's again in that moment of total weakness.

Lucy kissed Cameron on the mouth for a while, and then moved down to her neck. She loved the reaction it caused from Cameron. "I want you," Lucy whispered, her voice sounding raspy to her own ears.

"Lucy, oh my god." Cameron sat up and shifted away from her. "You're killing me here…"

"Cameron, I know you want me, too."

"Not here. Olaf can come down any minute."

"Yeah. You're right."

Lucy climbed off the hammock and walked to the side of the boat. She needed to cool off. Cameron came to stand right up against her from behind, her breath warm on her skin at the nape of her neck. Cameron's arms reached around her and hugged Lucy against her. Her voice was a mere whisper in her ear. "Are you okay?" She leaned her head on Lucy's shoulder, and Lucy could feel Cameron's body relax when she sighed.

Lucy giggled. "I came to stand here to cool off, and you standing so close to me is not helping."

"You deserve to be treated like a queen." Lucy could feel Cameron smile into her shoulder and looked back at her.

"I'm okay with whatever you want to do," Lucy said.

"Then come back to the hammock."

The rocking of the boat soon had them both drifting off. Not only out to sea, but also off to dreamland.

CHAPTER ELEVEN

"Dinner is ready."

A soft voice woke her from a deep and restful sleep. She frowned as she opened her eyes, only to find that it was dark already. She must have slept a few hours, at least.

"What time is it?" Lucy asked as she looked around, confused. It took her a few seconds to realize where they were still on the oversized yacht.

"It's seven pm. You slept all day." Cameron spoke softly.

"Oh my god. Are you serious?" She pulled herself from the hammock. "Let me go freshen up first. I guess I should take a quick shower." She yawned.

"I also took a shower while you were asleep. The water is nice and warm. Don't take long. The food is going to spoil."

"What are we having?"

"You packed it, remember? Caviar, salmon, cheese and crackers. I'll pour the wine. Hurry, I'm starving. This was supposed to be lunch, not dinner."

Lucy rushed into a cabin, took a hot shower, and found a travel toothbrush. When she was done, she donned her dress and returned to the deck. Cameron had laid out a beautiful table, complete with candlelight and wine glasses. She was seated by the table, sipping on a glass of white wine.

"What are you having?" she asked as she occupied the other chair.

"Chardonnay. Want some?" Cameron lifted the chilled bottle on the table and poured some into her glass.

"Wow. You went to so much trouble. Why didn't you wake me earlier?"

Cameron laughed. "I tried. You were so fast asleep, that you didn't even realize we're docked at the pier. Olaf left two hours ago. Eventually I got bored, so I set the table. Lucky for you I didn't have to cook anything."

"Your cooking is great."

"You've only tasted my eggs."

"Is that all you can make?"

"Not at all. Connie actually taught me how to cook. I'll make you dinner some time." Cameron chuckled.

Lucy watched as she built a cracker with cheese and caviar. Cameron popped it into her mouth and made a very sexy sound in her throat.

"You make me wish I was that cracker," Lucy said.

"Here, try this." Cameron made her the same combination of toppings and reached over to feed it to Lucy.

Lucy opened her mouth wide, trying to fit the entire cracker into her mouth. She managed to nibble on Cameron's fingers, too.

Cameron smirked. "Trying to eat my fingers, too?"

"Mm. That's delicious," Lucy said after she had swallowed. She watched in amazement as Cameron popped more food into her mouth.

"I can see you're hungry."

"Hey, I'm not the one who slept my butt off all day."

"Is that what I did?" Lucy looked at her backside. "Nope, it's still here."

"Yep, and still extremely sexy," Cameron purred. "Want to stay here tonight?"

"On the yacht? We didn't bring any clothes."

"Who said anything about wearing clothes?"

Lucy's stomach twisted as she imagined their naked bodies entwined, aching to satisfy and be satisfied. "You're really making this hard for me, you know," she growled.

"In that case I'm succeeding."

They ate in silence for a while, and when Lucy was full, she took a sip of her wine, placed her glass down and inhaled sharply. "Cameron... I think I'm falling for you."

Cameron nearly choked on her wine. "You are?"

"Like I've never experienced before. This is new to me. I don't know what to do."

Cameron reached across the table and placed her hand on top of Lucy's. "Lucy..." She took a deep breath in and exhaled slowly. "I love you."

Lucy took a large sip from her wine glass. She watched as Cameron got up and walked over to where she sat. Cameron took her glass from between her fingers and placed it down on the table. Her hands found Lucy's, and she pulled her gently to her feet. Their bodies met immediately, and Cameron's arms found their way around her waist. She kissed Lucy gently, her lips teasing her mouth slowly, leaving Lucy's body trembling for more.

"Fuck," Lucy said as her last inhibitions left her body. She deepened her kiss, and pulled Cameron's body as close to her as she could. Cameron's mouth hungrily responded to her lips, and she pushed herself into her, surrendering herself to Cameron completely. Lucy's hands slipped in under Cameron's shirt and she dug her nails into her back. She felt the muscles in Cameron's back contract. With one quick movement, she pulled Cameron's top over her head, and felt her hot skin as she held her in her arms. Their lips met once again, and they felt wonderfully familiar. Lucy knew

236

Cameron's breathing was going to quicken the instant her tongue found hers, and it did. Cameron's hands moved behind her neck and pulled her face hard against hers. Lucy felt Cameron's body tremble with need. Cameron snuck her fingers under Lucy's short dress and her hand froze when she found Lucy had no bra or bikini top on. Cameron pulled Lucy's dress over her head and when their bodies met again, Lucy felt her hard nipples pushing into Cameron's soft skin. Lucy's fingers found Cameron's bikini strap and she undid the clasp, letting the piece of garment drop to the floor. She moved her left hand to Cameron's chest and groaned when she found the tender skin of her breast.

Cameron pulled her face away from Lucy's and whispered, "Let's move this inside."

She entwined her fingers with Lucy's and pulled her into the lobby. Inside, the lighting was soft, and for the first time Lucy heard music coming from the iPod docking station. It was her playlist that she had sent Cameron a few weeks back. When they reached the huge L-shaped couch, Cameron nudged her gently and she dropped down onto the settee. As Lucy leaned backward, Cameron toppled on top of her. Her body felt great on Lucy, and their hips immediately started moving in slow unison. The familiar throbbing started a flame between Lucy's legs, and she arched her hips upward, savoring every movement as she gasped for air. Cameron's groin had immediately found the right spot, and Lucy's hands pulled Cameron's hips into her, intensifying the deepness of the pressure. Cameron's lips found hers again, and Lucy bit her lower lip gently, sucking Cameron's tongue into her mouth.

Cameron pulled away for a second and kissed her down her neck. She reached Lucy's nipple and sucked it into her mouth. Lucy's hands moved over Cameron's back and she dug her nails into her once more.

"Cameron. Please. I need you," she practically begged.

Cameron slid her hands down and removed Lucy's bikini bottoms. They were slick with her juices. She was entirely naked, completely exposed. She placed her fingers between Lucy's legs and hissed between her teeth, "Fuck, you're so wet."

"Take off your pants," Lucy said. "I want to touch you, too."

While holding herself up with her right arm, she used her left to pull her jeans down with her bikini bottoms. Lucy helped, and after a short struggle, they dropped the clothing items to the floor.

They were both naked now, and Lucy's heart bruised her ribcage the way it hammered away inside of her. "I want to taste you," Cameron said. Lucy opened her legs and guided Cameron's head down. Cameron's mouth sank into her lower lips and she licked up her juices.

"You taste so fucking good," she murmured before continuing a slow devouring of Lucy's tender skin. Lucy placed her hand on Cameron's head, for a short moment, but due to the weeks of foreplay, she was way too excited and wasn't ready for it to end so quickly.

"Wait," Lucy breathed.

Cameron looked up. "Want me to stop?" she asked.

"I am too close. I want to taste you, too," Lucy said as she sat up and moved over Cameron, so that Cameron was laying beneath her. Lucy kissed Cameron down her neck and nibbled, knowing what it did to her.

Cameron moaned. "You're driving me crazy, Lucy," she muttered.

Lucy kissed every inch of Cameron's skin, down her neck, to her breast. When her mouth reached Cameron's nipple, she paused before kissing and sucking Cameron's nipple. Cameron's fingers dug into Lucy's shoulders, and she cried out in pleasure. Lucy moved lower, taking her time, enjoying the effect she had on Cameron's movements. She could feel Cameron tensing and becoming breathless with want. Lucy toyed with her tongue all the way down until she reached between Cameron's thighs. Cameron parted her legs and lifted her pelvis to meet Lucy's mouth. Lucy made love to Cameron, licking up her wetness and savoring every inch of her. Cameron tasted so good, Lucy wanted more. She slid a finger inside of Cameron's folds, loving the warmth washing over her fingers. She played with her tongue over Cameron's clit and heard Cameron moan. She licked and sucked until she heard Cameron groaning and begging for her to kiss her. Lucy moved up to Cameron's face again and they kissed deeply, moving their bodies as one. Their hips moved together, their clits sliding over each other.

"Fuck. Yes," Cameron whispered.

Lucy placed her hand between them, using her fingers to stimulate Cameron's most sensitive spot. Cameron felt so good. So perfect. She had wanted her for so long, and it was finally happening. Lucy moved in slow movements, watching Cameron's face as she was reaching closer to climax, but not taking her over the edge.

"Please, please." Cameron bit her ear as she begged for release.

Lucy inserted a finger, using the palm of her hand to press against Cameron's center. With her hips, she moved against her hand, bringing them both closer to the edge. Cameron dug her fingers into Lucy's butt and pulled her closer, while thrusting with her hips in the rhythm of Lucy's movements.

The muscles in Lucy's butt clenched with every thrust, as she moved deeper and deeper inside Cameron with every movement. She kissed Cameron's face, her shoulder, her neck.

"God, Lucy. You feel so good," Cameron muttered.

"I'm all yours, Cameron," Lucy said into her ear.

Lucy kept moving at an unhurried pace, until she felt the pulsating orgasm build from deep within. Her body met Cameron's movements, as she pressed her fingers deeper into Cameron. She could feel Cameron tense, trying to hold back. Lucy slowed but Cameron begged her not to stop.

Lucy's body shattered as she climaxed. She could feel Cameron tightening around her fingers, as she came too. Their bodies moving as one, not slowing until the intensity started dying down and their muscles started to relax. Lucy finally collapsed into Cameron's arms and rested her head on her shoulder as she tried catching her breath.

"Wow, you really are amazing," Cameron breathed. She moved her hands over the front of her and played with Lucy's nipple.

Lucy stroked Cameron's hair. "So are you." She closed her eyes. She was in paradise. She could feel Cameron's heart still thumping against her chest, and she knew she truly loved her.

"You can't possibly still want to sleep." Cameron smiled at her.

"I have never felt so relaxed in my entire life," Lucy said with her head resting on Cameron's shoulder, and Cameron had her arm draped around Lucy's back. They lay like that for a few minutes, and after a while, when Lucy lifted her head to look at Cameron, she saw that she was fast asleep. It felt so good lying in Cameron Bishop's arms. Cameron's even breathing and the soft rocking of the boat soon lulled Lucy to sleep.

†

It was morning when Lucy woke. The rhythmic movement of the boat over the ripples on the water, and the hot sun woke her. She felt refreshed when she opened her eyes. Cameron stirred when she got up quietly but carried on sleeping. She looked down at Cameron. Her long brown hair lay splayed over the cushion, and she looked so peaceful, Lucy didn't want to disturb her.

Up on deck, their leftovers were still on the table. After she cleared up the mess, she went to the kitchen in order to get some coffee brewing. While the percolator set to work in making their coffee, she slipped off to the bathroom for a shower. By the time she returned, the coffee was made, and she poured two cups. Luckily someone had stocked up on long-life milk, because Lucy liked milk in her coffee. Cameron was still sleeping, so she left her mug on the coffee table, while she took hers up on deck. She could quite easily live like this. Just Cameron and her on their yacht. Sailing off into the sunset. Lucy finished her coffee and went to the kitchen for more. On passing the sofa, she noticed that Cameron was not in it anymore. In the kitchen, she refilled her cup, and then went searching for Cameron. She found her in the shower Lucy had used earlier, and she watched every magnificent detail of her perfect body when she raised her arms and massaged shampoo into her scalp. Cameron's eyes were closed, so she hadn't noticed Lucy. Lucy inched closer and continued enjoying the show. Cameron stepped back into the spray, her nipples hardening as the water glistened down her body.

"Uhum," Cameron cleared her throat.

Lucy looked up at her face and saw that she had opened her eyes.

"You can join me if you want."

"I've already showered." She giggled, but quickly undressed and stepped in with her.

Cameron's hands immediately reached for her, and she pulled Lucy close for a long kiss. "Good morning," she said. "This is how I'd like to wake up every morning."

Lucy pushed Cameron's back into the shower wall and kissed her neck, nibbling, gently biting her skin. She loved the sounds Cameron made every time she did that. Slowly, Lucy moved her mouth lower, over her nipples and down to her pelvis. Lucy dropped down to her knees and looked up at Cameron. The look in Cameron's face was a giveaway that she was all hers. Lucy could do with her as she wished. Lucy slid her fingers between Cameron's legs and felt that she was warm and wet, ready for release. Slowly, she teased with the tip of her tongue, and watched as Cameron's clit pulsated every time she moved away. She teased her for a long time before she finally sucked her into her mouth, while rolling her tongue in circular motions. Lucy could feel her clit throb in her mouth and knew she was aching for release. She didn't want it to end, so she reduced her pace. Cameron moaned and placed her hand on Lucy's head, pulling her closer. Lucy used more pressure and increased her pace. She felt Cameron move with her and heard her breathing increase rapidly. She slid a finger inside her and then another. While moving her fingers slowly, she continued her movements with her mouth. It didn't take long before she heard Cameron moaning, begging her not to stop. Lucy obeyed and continued until she felt Cameron clenching around her fingers and the juices flowing down her wrist. Lucy kept on until Cameron pulled her up and closed the faucet.

"My turn," Cameron said. She took Lucy by her hand and led her into the cabin. "Lie down," she instructed.

Lucy followed orders and did exactly what Cameron told her to do. The next moment, Cameron was on top of her, kissing Lucy with a passion she had never felt before. She needed Cameron more than she needed air. Cameron kissed her with fervor and placed her hand against Lucy's aching need. She entered her with two fingers and made love to her until Lucy couldn't stand it any longer. Lucy cried out as she came, while holding onto Cameron, afraid of letting go.

Cameron continued kissing her with a deep passion, as if devouring her soul. "I love you," she said over and over again as she kissed her, all over her face, neck, and breasts.

CHAPTER TWELVE

It had been a week since the enchanting night and morning on the yacht. Lucy found herself spending every night in Cameron's embrace, their love growing with each passing day. They reveled in the bliss of their intimate moments, feeling more alive and content than ever before.

As they finished their breakfast one morning, a call interrupted their peaceful moment. Cameron hurriedly answered the phone and stepped outside, her face clouded with concern. Lucy observed her from the window, watching as she paced nervously in the garden. After a few minutes, Cameron ended the call and made her way back inside.

"That was the hospital," Cameron uttered with a heavy sigh. "My dad had a fall and broke his hip. I need to go to the UK for a couple of days."

Lucy gasped, worry etching across her face. "Is he alright?"

"He's going for surgery tomorrow. I want to be there when he wakes up," Cameron replied, her voice filled with apprehension.

"Is there anything I can do? Can I come with you?" Lucy asked, eager to support Cameron during this difficult time.

"I would appreciate that, but your mom's will..." Cameron trailed off, her fingers tapping on her phone as she searched for available flights.

Lucy furrowed her brow, feeling a surge of determination. "What was my mom thinking? I'm sure we can talk to the executor and figure something out." She rummaged through a drawer, searching for the executor's business card. "Let me give him a call."

Cameron continued scrolling through flight options on her phone. "I found a flight departing this afternoon. Should I book two seats?"

Lucy dialed the number on the card, but it continued to ring unanswered. "They must be closed over the weekends," she muttered in disappointment. She turned to face Cameron, resolve in her eyes. "You know what, Cameron? I think it's best if you go ahead. If you need me, I'll be on the first flight out. I promise."

Lucy walked over to Cameron, embracing her tightly. Cameron held onto Lucy, as if seeking strength. With a soft exhale against Lucy's shoulder, Cameron whispered, "I'll go pack then."

Leaving the kitchen, Cameron headed toward her room, preparing for her trip. Lucy stood in the wake of her departure, the weight of the situation sinking in. Determined to support Cameron through this trying time, she vowed to join her as soon as possible.

†

The first night alone was excruciating. The second night was even worse than the first.

Lucy couldn't help but wonder how she was going to survive without Cameron until she returned. Cameron had called her when she arrived, and again from the hospital. Her father was fine, but he would need rehab after the time spent in hospital. Lucy had suggested she bring her dad home, but Cameron explained that her father was too weak to fly. Besides, she told Lucy, her dad had met a lovely lady and was in a serious relationship. It would be too complicated bringing him, or them home.

The entire time while Cameron was gone, Lucy had the distinct feeling that she was being watched. She tried suppressing the feeling of impending doom, but she kept hearing unexplainable sounds around the house, making her feel jumpy and even scared. There was even a moment when she thought it was the ghost of her mother, but she shrugged it off and told herself she was being ridiculous.

On the fifth night, as she lay in Cameron's bed, breathing in her lingering scent, Lucy wished she had gone with her. Cameron needed her, and she felt powerless. Two days previously, she had finally reached the attorney who was managing the estate, and Brett had informed her that her mom's testament stated that she wasn't able to leave for a year. He was merely following protocol. Lucy sighed into Cameron's pillow and longed for her arms, her lips, her voice. How had she survived all those years alone? Had she known what it was like sharing her life with someone else, she wouldn't have been single for that long. She smiled at the thought. No one could possibly take Cameron's place. She rolled onto her right side and curled up into the blankets. A short while later, she started drifting off to sleep.

Thump.

Lucy opened her eyes.

Thump.

She sat up and with shaky fingers, searched for the lamp switch. There was no one in the room. With shaky legs, she raised herself off the bed and rushed to the door. She opened it just a crack. The hallway was dark. Her heart raced as her mind began to conjure up all sorts of terrifying possibilities. Unwilling to succumb to fear, Lucy took a deep breath and reminded herself that there could be a logical explanation for the sound. With cautious steps, she tiptoed out of the room and descended the stairs, her senses on high alert. Each creak of the floorboards seemed magnified in the stillness of the night.

As she reached the ground floor, she nearly tripped over something on her way to the front door. She yelled out in surprise as she crouched down next to the apparently lifeless body on the floor. She turned his face up and saw it was Robert. The butler.

"Robert?" She desperately felt for his pulse. It was weak. Just as she tried to turn him on his back, she remembered her phone was upstairs. Hesitant but determined, she ran back up to Cameron's room. She had to call for help. Her phone wasn't there. Where had she left it? A third thump echoed through the house. Lucy's heart skipped a beat, and a shiver ran down her spine. She heard footsteps running up the stairs and with dread, she slipped inside Cameron's closet. She was breathing heavily and had to place her hand over her mouth in order to be quiet. She could see his shoes through the slats. He was inching closer to the cupboard doors. Lucy shifted back and the inside wall of Cameron's closet gave way. She fell back with a thud that winded her. She looked around her in a frenzy. She was in a secret passage. There were narrow stairs going down into a dimly lit room. Not knowing if her assailant had heard her falling through the closet wall, she quickly sprang down the stairs and found a hidden room. There was a bed, a lamp, and a bar fridge. Someone had been living there. Lucy saw a desk with a whole bunch of computer monitors, with every room on display. Someone had been watching them. In the shower, when they made love. Her heart was beating loudly now, and she knew she had to get away. There were multiple doorways exiting from the room and she decided to take the closest one.

A sharp stab in her neck caught her completely off guard. Her hand shot to the spot which had just been jabbed and her fingers wrapped around a plastic tube. She pulled it out. It was a syringe. Lucy collapsed to the ground. Before she even had a chance to comprehend the situation, her brain whirled into darkness.

She had no idea how long it was before she regained consciousness, but when she opened her eyes, she was tied up. Her hands were bound in front of her, and her feet were tied together. Before she could try free herself, she felt a sharp pain in her head. Someone was pulling her by her feet and her head was bouncing on the cobblestone. She tried to resist and kick with her feet, but he was stronger than her. She looked around and saw that they were on their way toward the edge of the cliff. What used to be her favorite spot would soon become her most dreaded. She knew what her perpetrator had in mind, so she started kicking with both legs, trying to grab onto something, anything in their path. The cobblestones were too sleek, and her hands were tied.

A male voice shouted at her, "Keep still or I'll break both your legs!"

His voice sounded vaguely familiar, but Lucy couldn't place it. She tried to get a good look at him, but it was difficult with the movement, and it was too dark to get a good look. He continued dragging her toward the edge of the cliff, and the cobblestone path scraped into her flesh as he kept at it. She tried to lift her head, so that it wouldn't bump on the hard ground while being dragged to her doom, but found that when she lifted her head, more pressure on her shoulders caused excruciating pain to the flesh over her shoulder blades. She cringed in pain, but decided not to kick him again, for fear of having two broken legs.

She recalled watching a video in nursing college on how to deal with psychologically unstable patients in the psychiatric hospital where they had part of their training. They were taught to talk to the assailant, try keeping them calm.

"Why are you doing this?" Lucy managed to ask while still being dragged to her final destination.

"People like you just don't get it, do you?" He breathed hard but continued down the path.

"Get what? I don't understand?"

He stopped. Lucy was grateful for the short break so that she could try and position her nightie back down slightly. It had moved all the way up to her shoulders due to the friction and had left her entire body exposed.

"You've always had everything your little heart desires." He looked down at her and she swallowed hard when she recognized him.

"Dick?"

He continued, "All my life, I had nothing. My parents were poor. I had to work my way through school. No pampered life for me, was there?"

"Dick. I am so sorry. How can I help? Is it money you want?" She felt his grip tighten around her ankles. "I have money, I can give you whatever you want."

"I'm gonna have it all. Everything. Up to the very last coin." He started down the path again, pulling her along. Her nightdress almost immediately found its way up her torso again, exposing her to him, and the tiny little stones on the cobblestone path were slicing into her skin.

"Dick. I don't understand what you're doing." She was desperate to distract him and to hear his deluded plan. She clenched her teeth in agony while she spoke. And for the first time she was glad that Cameron had left, otherwise Dick might have hurt her, too. She would rather die than see Cameron get harmed or killed. The last thought made her gulp.

"Ah. That's where my fiancé comes in. Frankie."

They had finally made it to the cliff. Not that Lucy wanted to be on that edge at that specific moment in time, but she couldn't handle the dragging anymore. She was sure that the flesh on her back was bleeding, but she couldn't feel with her fingers, because her hands were tied in front of her. With some effort, she managed to sit up.

"You guys are engaged?" She remembered the ring she had found in Frankie's drawer. "I don't understand how Frankie fits into the picture."

"Which is why we need you gone. You see, when you commit suicide by jumping down the cliff, the whole estate will be signed over to Cameron. And seeing as Cameron has always loved Frankie, they will be a couple. You know, eventually get married."

Lucy realized that he was completely psychotic. Living in a fantasy world.

"After Cameron marries Frankie, she will be entitled to everything when Cameron dies. So, I get rid of Cameron, and voila, deal done and dusted. Place is ours. Fool proof plan." He laughed the evilest laugh she had ever heard. It echoed down the cliff. "Of course, everything will take time, but as usual, Dick has to work for everything he gets. No. Nothing is ever free for Dick."

"Wow, you really thought this through. And the threatening notes? That was you, wasn't it?"

"Everything was me. I wanted you to leave before your mother left the estate to you. You were the only kink in my plan. When you arrived, I knew I had to get rid of you before your stupid lousy mother changed her mind about leaving the entire estate to Cameron. And then she did what she did, her whole stupid fifty-fifty scam. My last resort was to kill you."

"Did you poison me, too?" Lucy asked.

He fidgeted nervously with his hair. "That was easy. At the restaurant, your coffee. The stuff is called oleander. It's a very poisonous plant. I dropped a little bit of the nectar in your coffee without anyone noticing. You were so focused on Cameron and Frankie so close together that you never even noticed. Only, it was supposed to kill you. I don't know how you survived it. Maybe I didn't put enough of it in." He shook his head, looking sad. "Maybe next time."

"What did you inject me with now?" Lucy asked, hoping it was not some or other slow acting poison or something.

"Propofol, otherwise known as Diprivan. It is a short-acting anesthetic induction drug. I want it to be out of your system before I chuck you over the edge. Don't want any autopsies done now, do we?"

"But the police are going to investigate, you know that, right? They always do when there is a large amount of money involved."

He slapped his head. "Stop getting into my head," he bellowed.

Lucy tried to buy more time. "You still haven't told me all your genius work yet. How did you get the notes into my room? I didn't see you, you were good." Lucy tried to entice him, so she could buy some time, trying to come up with an escape plan. She suddenly remembered the hidden passage and room she had found before he had stabbed her with the syringe.

He chuckled. His laugh sounded crazy, and it made Lucy's stomach churn. "That's the best part. I was here all the time. I lived inside your house."

"But how did you manage that with all the servants, without being seen?" She already knew the answer. It wasn't hard to figure that part out.

He sat down on her rock. If her hands were not tied, she would have killed him right there and then. How dare he sit on her rock? "Remember I am the architect who did the renovations here? I built secret passages throughout the house. I can access any area from within the walls, without being seen." His insane eyes glittered in the moonlight.

Lucy's skin crawled at the thought of him in her house all this time. That was probably why she had been feeling watched. The thought of him watching her with Cameron, in their most intimate moments, made her cringe.

She had to keep the conversation going. She had no idea how she would get herself out of her current situation, but there had to be a way, and buying time was the best thing she could come up with now. "You're so clever, Dick." She spoke with a gentle tone. "How and where did you enter my room?" She hoped she could keep him talking. She was not ready to be thrown over the edge and plummet to her death. Not before she told Cameron she loved her. All the chances

255

she'd had, to tell Cameron how she felt and she never did. Lucy became angry at herself. Life was so short, and here she was, preserving her stupid self. She suddenly didn't mind dying, but not before she told Cameron how she really felt.

Dick continued talking about his "genius" plans. He seemed so proud of himself, and so happy that someone was interested in his sadistic ideas.

"I can enter from the back of your closet. There's a secret passage that I have created, that passes the back of every single closet in the entire house. Do you have any idea how long it took me to do this without anyone noticing? And the funny part is, your mother paid me to do it, and she didn't even know. God, she was stupid."

"How did you enter and exit the premises without getting caught?" That part puzzled her. She had never seen him around. Never even knew he visited Frankie at the house.

"Through the basement. Did you know that there is a tunnel underneath the house that leads out to the forest next to the road? I could come and go as I pleased without anyone knowing."

"Is Frankie in on this?"

Just then, Lucy heard Frankie's voice behind her. "Dick, what are you doing?" she screamed, sounding anxious.

Frantically, Lucy swung around, searching where Frankie's voice had come from and saw her running toward them. When she reached them, she was out of breath.

Dick shot up from the rock and grabbed Lucy. "Stay out of this, Frankie," he spoke through gritted teeth. "I'm doing this for us. Like you told me to."

He grabbed Lucy and pulled her right up to the edge of the cliff, his eyes wild and angry.

Frankie stopped and froze, looking at him with confusion written all over her face.

"I thought that this is what you wanted." He looked like he was close to tears.

Frankie just stood there for a long moment, not saying a word. It was then that Lucy noticed Frankie had a hand behind her back, and when she pulled it out, she pointed the gun at them.

Dick pulled her in front of him, using Lucy as his human shield. Lucy fought back and pulled forward, trying to duck. Frankie pulled the trigger. The sound sent shockwaves through the air. The world seemed to hold its breath. Each second was filled with anticipation and dread. Lucy looked down. There was no entrance wound and no blood. Frankie had missed.

Dick's hot breath touched her ear and she cringed. Her heart pounding louder than the sound of the gunshot. She felt Dick lean backward, and twisted her head to see what he was doing. Blood oozed from his left shoulder.

"You shot me, bitch!" he shouted at Frankie.

Dick's grip was like a vice around her. He held her tight to his body and she felt him stepping backward, closer to the edge. Her heart slammed against her ribcage as she knew they were almost at the end. Another gunshot penetrated the air. This time louder than the first. She felt the gust of wind and it flew past her head. The next moment Dick slipped behind her and took Lucy with him. She felt herself falling.

CHAPTER THIRTEEN

Her hands grabbed frantically at the very first thing and managed to grip a piece of protruding rock. Pain shot up her arms as her fingers held on for dear life. She felt something tugging at her legs and managed to look down. Her eyes had adjusted to the dark and she could see Dick by her feet. The expression of fear pinched his face as he dangled while holding onto her. His weight pulling her down.

When Lucy looked up, she saw Frankie at the top, looking down at them.

"Help me, Frankie. Please…" She could feel her grip loosening as the strength in her fingers started to weaken.

An evil glint flashed over Frankie's face. "What a treat. I get to watch you die." She stood above Lucy, satisfaction in her eyes. "Cameron is mine. Once you're dead, she will run to my arms for comfort, and then we can finally be together. Everything will be mine. You lose, bitch."

Someone else tackled her and pushed her to the side. Relief washed over Lucy like a gentle wave, soothing her anxieties and quieting her racing thoughts. Someone was there to save her. Her fingers were getting numb. She was unable to hold on for much longer, especially with Dick trying to climb up her body. She could barely manage her own weight, let alone his.

"Help me!" she hollered.

The next moment, Cameron's frantic face appeared above her.

"Cameron?"

"Take my hands, Lucy!" she called. Cameron stretched out her right arm and Lucy knew she could reach her if she would just let go of the rock she had clung to, but her hands were bound by the wrists and if she let go, she would fall.

"I can't. My hands are tied."

"I'm going to take your hands. Do you trust me?" she asked.

Lucy could feel Dick's grip sliding and looked down at him.

Dick closed his eyes and let go. Lucy watched as he slipped and fell in slow motion. His body landed with a crash and ricocheted against the rocks all the way down, settling in the ocean below. The hungry waves immediately lapped at him, grateful for another life. His limp form slammed repeatedly against the rocks.

Lucy looked up at Cameron. With Dick's extra weight gone, she had a bit more strength. Also, seeing Cameron's face gave her new hope. "I trust you," she managed through her teeth.

Cameron reached down and grabbed her around her wrist. As Lucy let go, she was amazed at Cameron's strength, and submitted to her, allowing herself to be rescued. With superhuman power Cameron pulled Lucy up and over the ledge. When Lucy was safe, she lay down on the ground, panting, and closed her eyes. With shaky fingers, Cameron untied her hands and feet.

"You saved my life," she said, out of breath.

"Are you okay? Are you hurt? What happened?" Cameron's voice was filled with trepidation.

Lucy slowed her breathing and looked at Cameron. "How... When... What are you doing here? I thought you were with your dad?"

"I wanted to surprise you." Cameron's hands moved over Lucy's body as she inspected her scrapes and bruises. "I knew I shouldn't have left you here on your own." Cameron held onto her, kissed her face and her lips. "I heard the gunshot just as the taxi dropped me off. I thought I'd lost you..." Cameron kissed her again.

"I'm still here..." Frankie's sarcastic voice came from behind them.

Lucy shot up into a sitting position. "You! You tried to shoot me!"

"Babe," Frankie said and backed away. "She's lying... I tried to save her from Dick."

"What the fuck is wrong with you?" Lucy yelled.

The sound of police walkie-talkies rang down the path, and Lucy saw a couple of uniformed men approaching. One of them caught Frankie right before she tried to sprint away. Lucy watched as they cuffed her.

"Are you ladies okay?" Another police officer walked over to them.

"This is all very confusing." Lucy shook her head.

"Your butler called us. Sorry it took so long to get here."

Cameron helped Lucy up to her feet. "You're hurt. You need to get to the hospital."

"Not a chance," Lucy said and hugged her again. "Your timing is impeccable, by the way."

Lucy held onto Cameron for a while longer. She never knew it was possible to love anyone that much. After a few moments, she broke away from her embrace and walked over to the cliff. She looked down, and managed to see Dick, still floating in the water, crashing repeatedly against the rocks. She turned to Cameron and wrapped her arms around her once more. "I love you. With my whole being."

The look of tenderness in Cameron's eyes sent warmth spreading through her entire body. "I love you too, Lucy."

"What are you doing here?" Lucy slapped her playfully on the chest.

"My dad was doing well, and his new girlfriend fussed enough over him for me to leave. Gosh, you must see them. They look so happy."

"I'm so glad you're home."

"Couldn't survive one more day away from you," she said as she placed her arm over Lucy's shoulder and led her back to the house. "Let's get you cleaned up. The police can handle this."

†

After getting their statements, the police left. Robert was taken to the hospital via ambulance. It took most of the night to have all the formalities taken care of. It turned out that Dick was wanted for assault, murder, rape, and fraud. In the early hours of the morning, a helicopter came to fetch Dick's body.

CHAPTER FOURTEEN

It had been a few weeks since the ordeal. Robert was alive and well, and back with them. The police had come to collect evidence, and had removed clothing, photos, surveillance cameras, and a whole lot of other garbage that Dick had accumulated over time. They found incriminating evidence against Frankie, too, which would help keep her locked up for a very long time. It had been a hectic few weeks, with police in and out the entire time. Their whole house was practically treated as a crime scene. They were finally allowed back into their home, after spending several days of bliss on the yacht. The attorneys approved it for legal reasons, as it was part of the estate.

"Oh my god, you are so great in bed." Cameron sighed after they made love that morning.

They had moved into Cameron's bedroom full time, so that they wouldn't have to spend a single moment apart.

Lucy kissed Cameron on her lips. "I love you," she confirmed once again.

"I love you, too," Cameron replied with evident emotion.

"I had never in my wildest dreams imagined I would ever fall in love. You, my love, surpass my every expectation. If I ever imagined what a committed relationship was like, this outdoes every thought. Cameron, you're perfect in every way. I love you more than life itself."

"You're my life, Lucy."

Lucy sat up. "I have an idea that I'd like to discuss with you. Paul's husband, Alan, has a sister. Her name is Rose. She owns a ranch called Liberation Ranch. I want to sell my dad's company and invest with Liberation Ranch instead. They take in victims of abuse. It will be money better spent than what my dad did."

Cameron's lips curved upward. "You're such a sweet soul, Lucy. I think that's a wonderful idea. Let's do it."

Lucy smiled. "Want to make love again?"

Charlene Neil

Epilogue

Cameron came up the narrow stairway toward where Lucy sat on deck. "We're set," she said with a smile before she kissed Lucy leisurely.

They had spent all morning making love and were just about ready to set sail on their new adventure. It had been a year since Dick plummeted to his death, Frankie was taken to prison, and Lucy's mom's will was finally concluded. They had managed to stay in the house together for a year and the estate was now theirs.

"Do you think my mom wrote her will like that so that we would end up together like this?" Lucy asked.

"Absolutely. She knew we were made for each other."

"It was my mom's last wish."

"On that subject," Cameron said, and knelt in front of Lucy, holding Angela's old engagement ring. "Lucy, before your mom died, she gave me this and asked me to give it to you one day…"

"Yes," Lucy interjected.

"I would be the luckie—"

"Yes."

"Let me finish," she said and chuckled.

"Yes, a thousand times over."

With trembling fingers, Cameron placed the ring on Lucy's finger, kissed her, smiled broadly and got up.

"I have a ring for you too," Lucy said and rummaged through her backpack. "I was going to ask you when we were out at sea." Lucy took the ring out and stood in front of Cameron. "Will you wear my ring?"

"Yes," Cameron said with a broad smile. "I don't just want to wear your ring, I want to marry you, you silly woman."

Lucy slipped the ring onto Cameron's finger and then kissed her tenderly.

"Are we going to put our skippers' licenses to good use?" Cameron asked.

"Most certainly, my love. Are you ready to see the world?"

"Couldn't be more ready," she said and turned to start the engines. "To the U.S.?" she asked.

"America, here we come."

267

ABOUT THE AUTHOR

<u>Charlene Neil</u> is a bisexual author based in Cape Town, South Africa, where she resides with her family. With a wild imagination that often transports her to parallel universes, Charlene has always been captivated by the power of storytelling. Having nurtured her love for writing from a young age, she discovered her passion for crafting poetry during her school years and later gained experience in songwriting as a member of her high school music band. While Charlene pursued a career as a nurse, her literary aspirations remained fervent.

In her leisure time, Charlene indulges in her love for the outdoors through hiking, riding her quad bike, camping, and finding inspiration in the breathtaking landscapes of her native South Africa. She also finds solace in the pages of books, immersing herself in a variety of genres and styles that fuel her creativity. Above all, the support and company of her family are of utmost importance to her, always cherishing the moments spent with her loved ones.

Charlene made her debut in the literary world with her first novella, "The Prodigins," which was published by Memories SA, a prominent South African publishing house catering to young readers. This imaginative work showcases Charlene's ability to captivate and connect with her audience through vivid storytelling and relatable characters. Following this success, she ventured into the realm of paranormal romance with her novel, "The Presence," published by Affinity Rainbow Publications. This book offers a unique blend of the supernatural and a heartwarming lesbian love story.

Continuing her exploration of diverse themes and genres, Charlene's novel, "Mom's Last Wish," unfolds as a gripping mystery interwoven with a tender lesbian romance. Readers are transported into a world where love, loss, and intrigue converge, highlighting Charlene's versatility as an author.

Currently, Charlene is diligently working on her upcoming novel, "Liberation Ranche." With the passion and dedication that have become her trademark, she aims to complete this work in 2024, anticipating its submission for publication. As her writing journey unfolds, readers can expect more enthralling tales that delve into various facets of life, love, and the power of the human spirit.

Charlene Neil is a passionate storyteller who thrives on creating immersive worlds and unforgettable characters. Through her writing, she seeks to inspire, entertain, and touch the hearts of readers across the globe.

Contact details:
e-mail: Charlene.neil@rocketmail.com

OTHER AFFINITY BOOKS

The Next Generation by Annette Mori

Despite Toni's legendary brilliance, even she could not stop the march of time. After learning her daughter, Joy, and Joy's two best friends, Pepper and Alina, attempted to deceive the senior agents in The Organization with a bogus Spring Break cover story, she convinces her wife it's time to let the Next Generation take over.

The last thing Pepper Maggio expects after agreeing to lead a mission is literally running into the woman she's followed for years. Not only is Grace Turner beautiful, but she's a passionate crusader for the same innocents that The Organization vows to protect. Along with her two best friends, the three young women embark on an adventure to save the day. But the mission quickly gets out of hand as the human traffickers target not only Grace and her film crew, but also the young Mexican woman who managed to catch Alina's eye. Maria might be the bravest of the bunch as a survivor of one of the Mexican mines, but she's a sitting duck if they don't intervene. They might be the Next Generation, but they'll need the full support of The Organization, including Pepper's lethal mother, Val, to get out of Mexico alive.

Turn the Page by Ali Spooner
Continue the journey with Whit and Eli in this final installment of the Cast Iron Farm series. The brilliance of their twins, Mack and Zack, rapidly develops, challenging Whit and Eli to keep up with their education. Their sensitivity to others and kindness are far beyond their youth and a testament to the family's efforts to help them grow into young adults. In addition to more adventures, a budding romance, and wedding bells ring for the Fortner family once more as a new generation begins life on Cast Iron Farm.

A Breath of Scandal by S Anne Gardner
Adele Visconti, Contessa de Caravagio, is passionate and wild and doesn't know the meaning of the word no. One day by chance she turns her head and in a very old cliché fashion she sees a face across the expanse of a Polo field and goes to meet it. Unknowingly this would change her life forever.

When Gillian meets Adele, she is in a committed relationship. The last thing she wanted was to be sucked into the maelstrom that is Adele. However, Adele was something that she could not fight against and her world was turned upside down from the moment they met.

Will their relationship survive against a tide of intrigue, manipulations, passion, family, and most importantly reconnecting the magic of their love for each other.

The Sky People by Ali Spooner

After a beautiful wedding, Eli and Whit return to plan the next phase of their relationship. Whit discovers the identity of her father, and he shares a future with her that will change life on Cast Iron Farm forever. Twins bless the Fortner family, and Eli shares a special secret with Mitch, who bonds with the children in a unique way. Ride along as the Fortners begin a new chapter of their story.

Love Bonds by Annette Mori

When Mila Thompson, a rookie police officer, discovers her mother is missing, she engages the assistance of San Diego's number one detective, who is more than a little reluctant to enter the fray, noting she works in homicide, not missing persons.

Bernie doesn't play well with others, which is why she doesn't have a partner at work or in her personal life. When Mila approaches her, she tries hard to refuse the request, but Mila will not accept no for an answer. For reasons she does not understand, Bernie doesn't want to say no to Mila, who can charm her way into anything, including smoothing the rough edges of Bernie's crusty heart.

Things get complicated when the women in The Organization have an unusual tie to Mila's mother. This sets up an action-packed adventure with twists and turns and a healthy dose of love. Find out the future of The Organization and whether an unlikely pair can find their way to love.

Holy Water and Whiskey Scars by Ali Spooner

Faith Wilson and Logan Bronson have family secrets to protect and a legacy to uphold to support their small rural Appalachian community. Their commitment to each other is strong, and their desire to aid the struggling families however they can, lead them both down an exciting but dangerous path. Will their love continue to grow and be the glue that binds the community together, or will they flee the withering community?

Politics of Love by Annette Mori

Governor Sandra Murphy is rethinking the sanity of allowing her mother to talk her into considering becoming the democratic party's choice for the presidential nominee. Sandra has enough to contend with after surviving a bomb attack, thanks to the brave border control agent working alongside the clever undercover FBI agent. Now she has to worry about a pesky reporter who seems to be everywhere scoping stories Sandra would prefer Wynter Holmes steer far away from.

Wynter admires the charismatic governor. After all, she voted for the woman. But that doesn't give Governor Murphy a free pass. A breaking story is what Wynter lives for, and she isn't about to stop digging just because the engaging governor is attractive, single, and an out lesbian. Reporting for the famously biased, right-wing media conglomerate is not exactly making Wynter a friend of the enigmatic leader.

Will repeated attempts on Governor Murphy's life where Wynter might be collateral damage bring them closer together or tear them apart from what might be a perfect match?

Out and Loud by Ali Spooner

The Bentleys have begun celebrating their success by performing live in small venues and outdoor concerts. Their music and love for one another continue to grow as their number drops to four. Stone is needed at home to run the business during his father's rehabilitation, but the Bentleys drive forward. Cedra's challenge to her bandmates to create original songs for their next album turns into brilliant love songs, rockabilly, and a Pride Festival anthem. Ride along with the Bentleys as they capture the hearts of country music lovers across the nation.

Undercover Love by Annette Mori

When the domestic terrorist cell Emma Schmidt has infiltrated summons her to an abandoned warehouse for a loyalty test, Emma immediately recognizes the battered woman. Emma must act fast to protect her cover and save the woman, Jimena Aguilar, she's never forgotten.

Emma and Jimena team up on a dangerous mission to take down the terrorist cell and save the life of the popular California governor.

Will this lead them back to the closeness they once shared or have the years in between hardened their hearts to love.

Changing Times by Jen Silver

Thirty years on from when we first met Dani Barker and Camila Callaghan in *Changing Perspectives*, they're enjoying marriage and semi-retirement in a luxury flat near London.

Dani's niece, Holly, runs their mixed media business, now gaining a foothold in the highly competitive online games market. Holly's older sibling, Luc, influences people to take action on climate issues with their website, Gaia One: One Earth, One Chance.

Romance has been in short supply for both Holly and Luc. Immersed in her work, Holly's dating life is non-existent. For Luc, family prejudices stand in the way of a relationship with the love of their life.

Can Holly and Luc succeed in making the changes necessary to achieve their own happy ever afters?

Midnight in Nashville by Ali Spooner

The Bentleys have successfully finished cutting their first album, *Six Strings, and a Dream.* When the Covid-19 epidemic hits, tours and live performances are cancelled as the world goes into lockdown. With the closing of the restaurant, employment for the band members has been severely impacted. The group comes together to make life work at Ma Bentley's Boarding House. They take advantage of their down time and use of the studio to record more songs. Cedra has challenged each of her bandmates to create a song for their next album. Juliet's song, "Midnight in Nashville," is chosen as the title track. Join the group as they venture into new marketing avenues and create their first music video for the title track.

Compound Interest by Annette Mori

The kick-ass women in The Organization are back and they have their sights set on a few new recruits. Not everyone is jumping for joy at the choices, considering subterfuge is front and center in the games the new recruits have been playing.

Dani is supposed to get her happily ever after, but she's not sure what's real anymore including Candy's feelings for her. When a new enemy takes Candy captive, Dani vows to uncover the truth by insisting on going on the mission to save her. Candy is not what she seems, and that presents a new set of complications for Dani and her feelings.

The Organization continues to have challenges when those damn book magicians and book witches keep popping back in to warn them of new catastrophes on the horizon. She doesn't have time for their warnings, until their enemies intersect once again to keep them working together.

From award-winning author, Annette Mori, find out what happens in this final chapter of the combined Asset Management/Book Addict series.

Affinity
Rainbow Publications

eBooks, Print, Free eBooks

Visit our website for more publications available online.

https://affinityebooks.com/

Published by Affinity Rainbow Publications
A Division of Affinity eBook Press NZ LTD
Canterbury, New Zealand

Registered Company 2517228

www.ingramcontent.com/pod-product-compliance
Lightning Source LLC
Chambersburg PA
CBHW051246260626
47162CB00002B/636